CW00498546

This is a work of fiction.
incidents are either the pro<
or are used fictitiously, a
persons, living or dead, bu:
locales is entirely coincidenta

Published by Stuart Kenyon 2020

For Vicky, Max and Poppy

Chapter 51 — Luke Norman — 00:10

Poor little bugger.

Luke smoothes a stray strand of hair from his unconscious son's head and listens to him breathe for a moment. The boy's never had trouble sleeping, even when he was a baby. Over the last couple of days, Connor's been through enough to fuel nightmares for life. Right now, though, despite being in a strange bed, in an admittedly spooky house, he's too exhausted to resist slumber's call.

Yawning, Luke considers climbing into the bed with his child. He's flagging, physically and emotionally. But his brain is wired, his thoughts a maelstrom. Therefore, he gives Connor a kiss on the cheek, the sort that would trigger indignant outrage were the boy awake. He slips out of the room and shuts the door, muffling the gentle snores from his kid and Evie in the top bunk.

The noise from the next bedroom is louder. Theo and Gabriela surrendered to fatigue an hour ago and are fast asleep in their bunks; Ashara's in a camp bed. From behind the next oaken door on the dim corridor, where Josh Gould and Floyd Nelson are quartered, comes the low buzz of conversation. The latter's voice isn't audible, only the educated tones of the former.

Either Floyd's not as tired as he looked earlier, or Gould is talking to himself. Which wouldn't surprise Luke. Most of the previous day was devoted to searching Mortborough for runaway children, so he's been kept away from the former bus station supervisor. The execution of Geraint on Monday and Gould's justification for pulling the trigger are stark reminders that the older man, as helpful as he was in recovering Connor on consecutive days, is volatile. Potentially dangerous.

And if Luke's learnt anything over the last forty-eight hours, it's that sometimes the living can pose as much of a threat as the dead.

The last room off the upstairs hallway leads to the red house's master bedroom. Lena's already within, asleep again after rousing for a while at ten o'clock. Jada, who's downstairs and taking the first watch, will share the master with the injured woman. They'll stay here for one night only. Leave at first light.

As he descends the staircase, he hears night time noises in the woods outside. *I 'ope they're outside, anyway.* Maybe Jada's gone out for some fresh air; it is close and muggy in the old red house. Reaching the blind corner at the bottom of the stairs, Luke sees the red lights; he's instantly transported back to his childhood. Just as he was when the survivors came upon the residence the previous evening.

His dad used to take him for walks in Salton Woods. They would take the dogs and ramble around the ancient forest, and the 'red house' was always their final destination. No more than two hundred and fifty yards from some of the most deprived tower blocks in Salton, the Victorian pile is well-known to locals. All of its interior lights are – and have always been – rose-tinted, lending the tree-surrounded building a foreboding air.

Although the lights were always on, young Luke must've passed the place dozens of times without seeing a living soul inside. The same applied when adult Luke and his ragtag band of refugees arrived yesterday. The canal was blocked by a grisly bulwark of bodies, a floating drift of the dead, their pale flesh dappled by the late afternoon sun. By that point, everyone was weary. So the secluded red house, seemingly untouched by the apocalypse raging across Greater Manchester, was a welcome sight.

A night's rest. Then we'll push on. Find somewhere safer, more remote. Like Dad's.

"Luke?" Jada's call makes him jump.

"Yeah?" He steps into the wood-panelled hall, notes the only open door, the smell of coffee against that of dust.

"In here." Her voice comes from the kitchen, which has the largest window. She gives him a tired grin when he joins her. Her afro hair is dishevelled, her caramel skin a touch paler than usual. She's still beautiful, though. Still cool, clever, gutsy, warm… perfect. *Wonder if I'll ever get the chance, or the balls, t' do somethin' 'bout it?*

Luke returns her smile. "Y'alright?"

"Good, but tired. You?"

"Same. Is that… my phone?" A black device is on the kitchen counter, plugged into a wall in place of a 1970s toaster.

"Yeah. It's the only one the charger here'll fit. Thought I'd switch it on. See if there's any news about… all this. You don't mind? Sorry, I shoulda asked —"

"'S ok, no probs. Show me."

"Can't. The charger's shit. Gave it about five percent then died."

"What does it say on the news, then?"

"Internet was really dodgy. Could only get on BBC. Official story is that this is a 'terrorist incident' which is 'under control'."

Luke chuckles mirthlessly. "What a loada bollocks. 'Ey, what 'bout the telly?"

"Already thought o' that. No reception."

"Weird."

Jada yawns, then rolls her neck.

"Sit down fer a bit. I'll keep watch."

"Ta." She sits at a breakfast bar with a sigh. "So. What next?"

He puffs his cheeks. "Fuck knows."

"Suppose we got two choices."

"Yeah?"

"Yeah. Sounds like your dad's place in the country would be a good spot to hide out. But there's the refugee camp Gould heard about, too."

"You forgot option three."

"What's that?"

Luke narrows his eyes. He's been staring out of the window at the driveway, the only access to the house, without really seeing the moonlit gravel track lined with firs and oaks. Was it simply his imagination, or did something flit across his line of sight? "Gould was rantin' on 'bout it."

She stands to look over his shoulder; for a moment, she's close enough to smell. "Goin' straight to London with 'the truth'?"

"Yeah. You still want to nail the Government, don't you?"

"Of course. Damn right. All those bodies in the canal… everything we've been through an' seen… could've all been prevented. People deserve the truth. An' those bastards in Whitehall need to pay."

"So 'ow do we make that 'appen? London, like Gould said?"

"Not yet. Survivin', an' makin' sure Lena survives, that's what we need to do for now."

"This is just me 'n' you talkin' now, though, innit? What does everyone else wanna do?"

"Well, the kids seem to have made their peace with the fact they won't find their parents."

"Yeah, they've learnt their lesson. The older kids, they're more sensible. They know we've got Floyd with us. They've seen 'im kickin' arse."

"So we don't have to worry about them runnin' off. Brad?"

"Think he's on board wi' your plan. He wants revenge, wants t' fight fer it 'imself, but he knows your way is best. What 'bout Ashara?"

"She just doesn't wanna be alone, so she'll do whatever the majority does. An' she wants to help. She's been great with Lena. Used to be a nurse, ya know." Retaking her stool, Jada nods to herself. "Leavin' Floyd an' Lena."

Again Luke squints into the darkness, for he's sure he just heard a twig snap. *Nothin'. Just chill, man.* "Floyd seems like a good guy. Still hates Lena, but I think he's dealin' with it. Reckon he's pretty attached t' Theo 'n' Gabriela, anyway. 'N' as for Lena, she's not in the shape to argue anythin' with anybody."

"She's gettin' worse. I know she was awake for a bit before, but I'm worried she'll get sepsis if we don't get that wound treated soon."

"See 'ow she is tomorrow. If she's the same, or worse, we should try 'n' get her some meds from somewhere in Salton before we try movin' 'er again."

"At least the bleedin's stopped now." Jada yawns like a cavern.

Luke puts a hand on her shoulder. There's strength there, but like everyone else, she's flagging. "Go 'n' get a bit of rest, Jada. I'll take first watch."

"I'm fine. 'Sides, you almost swallowed me with your last yawn!"

"I know. I'm tired too, but I feel wired. I ain't ready t' sleep."

"Sure?"

He nods.

"Okay, thanks. Gimme a shout if you need to swap before it's Floyd's turn."

"I'll be fine."

She turns to head back towards the hallway, then pulls up short. Stooping, she kisses him on the cheek.

He ignores the stirring in his loins and gives her a smile.

Then she's gone, her footsteps receding into the bowels of the building. Luke puffs his cheeks and pours himself some coffee. Suddenly, it's deathly silent in the old red house. He stands at the window, staring into the black of night.

Any o' them ugly motherfuckers show up, we'll be ready.

An assault rifle and Brad's axe are just feet away, on the opposite kitchen counter, but Luke feels better when he touches the weaponry. He sips his brew. Eyes intent on the big window, seeing nothing save the pebbled driveway and the closest trees. It's a moonless night, without even the faintest whisper of a breeze amongst the trees.

Anything could be out there. Zombies. Zombie dogs. Zombie birds.

Even so, his eyes are getting heavier. The coffee's not working; maybe it's decaffeinated. His chin finds a resting place, propped on his arms folded in front of him.

He imagines a full zoo of zombified animals: lions, hippos, penguins. All charging at the house, with skeletons riding zombie-horses at the rear.

Suddenly he's falling, but only in his dreams. He rouses with a gasp, shakes his head and gets up to walk around. Always with an eye on the drive-facing window.

Need t' stay awake. Everyone's relyin' on me stayin' wide awake. Maybe fresh air'll 'elp.

So he heads to the back door. He's got his hand on the handle, ready to twist, when a thought gives him pause. *They smell blood. If I'm out in the open, my blood'll smell stronger, right?*

"Fuck. Need to man up, Norman. Only a coupla hours. Then Floyd's turn."

He retakes his stool at the breakfast bar and plays a drumbeat on the forty-year old MDF. Once upon a time, Christmas if he remembers correctly, his parents bought him a drum kit, but his mother tired of the noise and sold it on eBay. How much did it sell for? He can't remember. In any case, he wasn't allowed to spend the proceeds.

Nodding again. And drooling, like a zombie dribbling blood from its latest kill. Sleep, warm and comforting like a blanket, is irresistible. He can't fight it because he wants it.

Now he's playing the drums for real. Connor's on the guitar, Jada the keyboard – she's hammering away like she's running out of time to submit an article. In fact, she *is* writing; her piano is attached to a monitor.

"What are you writing about?" Luke sings, punctuating the question with a gong. He plays a drumroll while waiting for an answer.

"What do you think I'm writing about?" she calls. "The zombies, obvs."

The zombies. *Wake up, Luke.*

Jada stops typing, stands and beckons Luke towards a door.

Dumbly, he follows her into a hotel bedroom. When she begins to undress, he does likewise, his hands fumbling at his belt.

"Come on." She has a hungry look on her face. She gets into the king-size bed, on top of the sheets. "It's not often we get away from the kids, is it?"

The kids? Our *kids?*

Suddenly they're both at the window, looking out onto the car park. There are no vehicles, just a vacant, gravelled yard surrounded by trees.

"Look!" Jada points: there are monsters amongst the dead vegetation. Rotting skeletons, their limbs as wasted as the tree trunks and branches. Flesh peeling from bone like the bark from the firs and elms.

Wake up, Luke. Fer fucksake, dickhead, wake up!

He comes to with a jolt. Winces at pain in his eye socket; he's been slumped across his arms, his knuckles an uncomfortable pillow.

That's the least of his concerns, however. A scraping sound outside has him up on his feet, his veins abruptly flooded by adrenaline. Day is breaking.

'Ow fuckin' long was I asleep?

The light's still faint, but he can see further than he could last night: all the way to the bend in the track fifty yards from the red house.

Again, noise outside. Luke thumbs grit from his eyes and stares into the undergrowth, but he spies nothing of interest. *Just yer imagination. Bad dreams fuckin' wi' yer 'ead.*

Leaning on the kitchen sink, he takes a few deep breaths. *Get a grip. Better go wake the others.*

Just as he turns away from the window, something flashes across his peripheral vision.

This time he sees. There's only one grotesque figure at first. A parody of an adult male, it limps along, right foot turned inwards, its right ear tucked into its shoulder, left hand outstretched. Then number two appears.

"Guys!" Luke continues to stare as more of the ghouls materialise at the bend in the track. "Guys! Get the fuck down 'ere!"

Chapter 52 — Floyd Nelson — 05:50

"Guys!" Gurdeep mouths the words, but not in his own voice. His lips, framed by jet black beard, move slowly, like he's underwater. Now he's turning away. Breaking eye contact.

Floyd feels a pain in his bosom, as though someone's kicked him. "No!" he shouts as his friend turns to dust.

"Guys!"

And Floyd's up on his feet. The dream is banished, and his conscious mind reasserts control.

Gould's stirring, reaching for his revolver. "The fuck's going on?"

The young soldier doesn't reply; he's already out of the bedroom, pistol in hand, heading for the stairs. *Dat fuckin' stink!*

Turning at a mezzanine, he passes a window and has to squint. *Already light. Why da fuck did no one wake me for my watch?*

Above him, doors are opening. Panicked chatter, much of it high-pitched. Someone calls, "Floyd," but there's no time to stop and talk. He's just stepped foot into the ground floor when Luke yells again. The stream of Mancunian and profanity is almost incoherent, yet one word is unmistakable. "Zombies!"

Worst case scenario: the enemy have already breached the red house, so Private Nelson works under that assumption, tactically-clearing the hallway with his gun ready to fire. Footsteps clatter on the wooden staircase to his rear. *Need to secure da area before da rest get down 'ere.* "Stay upstairs!" he calls over his shoulder.

He feels alive. He's ready for whatever lies in wait. *Every fuckin' ugly zombie bastard gonna die —*

"Floyd?" Luke's in the kitchen.

The soldier assesses the room in a heartbeat. His gaze lingers on the large window above the sink; a flurry of movement catches his eye. "'Ow many?" he demands without giving Luke as much as a glance.

"Dunno. Fifty? Maybe more? The first one I saw wondered off into the trees, but the rest're still comin'."

"Ya checked any o' da other rooms?"

"No. Didn't wanna take my eyes of these —"

"Good finkin'. Go 'ave a look now."

The other man takes a split second to think, then does as bidden.

As Nelson grabs the battle rifle taken from the MIBs at The Wharfstar, he overhears Luke talking to another man. More footfalls, some on the floorboards over his head, others on the stairs. Meanwhile, he's aiming the gun at the glass, using the sight to count his foes on the drive and dirt track. *Good countin', Luke.*

The Mancunian reappears in the doorway, with Josh Gould in tow. "Nothing," the former states. "Think they're all comin' this way."

They're getting nearer. As always, the beasts move at varying speeds. A suited, spectacled former female, her silver hair splattered crimson and her nose and top lip chewed off, leads the way. Its gait is curious: side-on with one arm behind the back, like a drunken Olympic fencer. Close behind is a child-zomb, its stumpy, grazed legs jerking marionette-style. They're twenty yards ahead of the bulk of the horde, which are still negotiating the trees and shrubs.

"We defo sure they're comin' this way?" Brad walks into the kitchen and loads a rifle.

"Looks like it." Floyd lips sweat off his tongue. "But we need to be sure, ya get me?" *I'm da soldier. I be givin' da orders.* "Brad. I want you front of house. In dat lounge. Big bay window. Jus' in case dey circle 'round. Right?"

The shorter man nods, his face grim.

"Gould. Ya got much spare ammo for dat ol' piece?"

The older fellow looks at his revolver as if the idea has never occurred to him. "No, I don't suppose I have."

"Take my pistol, den." He hands over his Glock and a spare clip. "I want you in the top window facing the drive. Wait till dey close enough so ya can't miss. Ya feel me?"

"I do."

"'Member, need to aim for da head, if poss."

"No shit." Luke's already squinting down the barrel of his rifle, which is protruding from the sash pane at the right-hand side of the window. "We ain't dumb, Floyd."

"Yeah. Probably killed more zombs than you." Brad's on his way out of the kitchen, and he passes Jada on the way.

"Don't think it's time for a dick-measuring contest, guys," she says, grabbing the last remaining rifle. She eyeballs Floyd. "Where d'ya want me?"

She got some fire in her, dat one. He grins and points to the kitchen-dining space, to their right, which has its own window looking out onto the driveway. "Dere, please. Good angle, ya get me?"

"Very good, Private Nelson."

I can do dis. I am *cut out for da Army. Not jus' as a grunt, but as a* leader. He joins Luke at the window, but at the opposite end, where a separate sash opens.

Silver-haired female zombie is now within ten yards, the little boy hot on its heels. To their rear, there's a whole football team, still wearing their club colours, though the brilliant white is stained with blood and filth. The rest are an assortment of construction workers, casually-dressed teens, pensioners. One common feature is that their clothes look wet.

Dey da ones blockin' da water. If we can kill 'em, get past 'em, we can get back in da boat.

The stench of rotting bodies, spiced by the dirty canal, grows stronger. Already, the day's getting warm.

"Let 'em get close, yeah?" Floyd glances at his comrades.

"Yeah." Luke's voice is tight. "Headshots."

"Right. I'll take dem on da left. Fire dead ahead, so we ain't shootin' da same ones twice. Make sure ya don't hit dose Calor gas canisters." *Shit, did I see some on da other side o' da buildin' too? Who da fuck 'as deir own gas bottles dese days?* "Need to conserve ammo. Don't know 'ow long we'll be 'ere…" *Ya ramblin', fam.* "Kids safe upstairs, yeah?"

"With Ashara," Jada says. "They've got the axe, sledgehammer an' shit."

Silver-hair's within spitting distance; the capital G on her designer belt glints in the early rays. There's a birthmark shaped like a sickle on the boy's mud-flecked cheek; he's accelerating. As are the footballers, who jostle for position and trip over one another's feet.

"Fire!" The serviceman squeezes his trigger and revels in the feel of the single shot. Luckily, the young lad wasn't in his line of sight – Floyd doesn't enjoy blasting minors, undead or not – so it's the business-dressed woman he leaves with a third red eye, centre of forehead. A mini-fountain of crimson spurts onto nose, mouth and chin. The fiend sinks to its knees as if in prayer.

While rounds are loosed to Floyd's right, he twitches the barrel of his weapon left to send a 7.62x51mm NATO slug through the cheekbone of Salton Town's goalkeeper. Then left again: a goth girl takes hers in the mouth, between her black-daubed lips. Spluttering scarlet, it falls face first onto crazy paving.

Someone's firin' bursts.

"Luke, bruv, single shots, ya get me."

"Get ya."

Dat's better.

One-by-one, the invading force is exterminated. Floyd misses one attempt out of fifteen or sixteen. The other two aren't quite as efficient, but given their lack of training, they perform admirably. Their commander calls shots when he's unsighted, gives praise when it's due and reiterates the importance of ammunition economy.

From the first floor, Gould's firing sensibly. Several of the attackers succumb to bullet holes through the top of their skulls.

No more than a minute has passed when the final freak, an obese, balding security guard, emerges from the trees. Three high-powered assault rifles swing to bear.

"Who's takin' dis fat bastard, den?" Floyd wants to land the coup de gras; he's enjoying himself more than he should.

Luke laughs. "Be my guest, mate."

"Definitely the last one?" Jada mops perspiration from her brow.

Nuttin' from Brad.

Luke levels his longarm. "I'll have the fucker, then, if no one —"

A clattering sound from the hallway distracts him, and the undead security officer loses an ear to the bullet.

Da fuck? "Jada. Stay 'ere."

With Luke close behind, Private Nelson reaches the hallway just as Jada fires. Brad's at the other end of the corridor, but he's obscured. Four scantily-clad, middle-aged zombies are in the way, the basement door still open behind them. Three lurch towards Floyd and Luke; the other goes the opposite way.

Knew we shoulda busted open dat basement.

Brad's already aiming. He fires, hitting a red-haired female in the chest. The lingerie-sporting abomination slumps against the wall.

Luke gasps. Cries out in fear more than pain: his friend's shot punched straight through the redhead zomb and grazed his arm.

"Kill dem, Brad!" Floyd seizes Luke by the scruff of his neck, drops, pulls the other man with himself.

Their friend opens fire. Hot metal whistles overhead, penetrating flesh, wood and brickwork; the noise is deafening in the enclosed space. Although Brad's burst lasts no more than a few heartbeats, Floyd says a silent prayer of thanks when it's over. After a quick glance confirms the demise of all four cellar-dwellers, he stands and looks down at Luke, who remains prostrate. "You good, bruv? He get ya bad?"

Sitting up, the white man gapes at his winged arm. There's no blood, merely a blackened tear in his shirtsleeve. "What? Where's the… Brad, ya prick, ya shot me!"

His buddy is stepping over the red house's double-dead occupants. "Fuck off! Where's the blood?"

"Look!" Eyes blazing, Luke brandishes his arm.

"I did ya a favour. That shirt's fuckin' awful." At first, he keeps a straight face, but then he begins to smirk.

Luke chuckles, as does Floyd.

"Sorry, bro," says Brad.

"Sorry for what?" asks Jada as she emerges from the kitchen. "What's so funny?"

The boys explain.

Jada exclaims and examines Luke's arm. "You were lucky. Another millimetre and you'd be like Lena."

"Speakin' o' Lena…" Luke looks at the stairs. "Has anyone checked her?"

Floyd glowers. *Fuck dat bitch. My boy Gurd dead 'cause o' her.* He goes back into the kitchen and stares at the carnage outside without actually registering the horror; instead, he sees his friend Gurdeep, dying on the canal towpath. He can still hear the others talking.

"No one's checked," Jada replies, "'cause we got a bit of a rude awakenin', didn't we?"

"Yeah. What the fuck happened, Luke?" Brad's voice gets fainter as he heads back to his post, in the lounge.

"Sorry, guys." Luke sounds embarrassed. "I just… I was so tired."

"We clear?" Gould's disembodied voice triggers a stab of recollection.

Dat crazy motherfucker was talkin' to hisself all fuckin' night!

Floyd shakes his head. He's in a weird old house that lights up red like a brothel at night, in the middle of a forest on the edge of one of the country's most deprived council estates.

His companions: Luke and Jada obviously want to have sex, which could prove a distraction; consumed by anger, Brad's like a reactor ready to blow; though intelligent, Ashara is not a fighter; Lena's a liability thanks to her injury; and as for Gould, apart from his idiosyncrasies, he murdered someone on Monday night. No doubt Geraint had it coming, abducting youngsters, yet who made Gould judge, jury and executioner? And regarding children, there are four of them upstairs. Two boys, two girls. They're good kids, but keeping them safe adds further stress to an already difficult situation.

Maybe I should leave. Walk away now, 'fore it's too late. He wants revenge for Gurdeep; if it weren't for the politicians Lena with whom Lena Adderley was involved, Floyd's friend would still be alive. But how realistic are Jada's hopes of exposing the Government? Will they even survive long enough?

He continues to stare out of the window, ignoring conversation between Luke, Jada and Gould, who have re-entered the kitchen. A flicker of movement among the trees piques his interest. *Shit. More o' da stinkin' fuckers.* He uses the scope on his stolen rifle to scan the woods.

"'S up?" asks Jada.

"More zombies." Floyd closes his eyes for a moment. "A lot more."

She hefts her weapon and copies him, then winces. "Left and right, as well as dead ahead."

"We be surrounded soon. Need to fall back."

"Those flats are just a coupla hundred yards away," Luke reminds them.

"Let's go, den. Gould, go get da kids down 'ere. Ashara too."

"What about Lena?" Jada has hands on hips. "We're not leavin' her behind."

Fuck. Floyd storms out, heading the lounge. Barely registering the giant tiger skin rug and the abundance of brass ornaments, he relays the news. He studies the woodland to the property's front as Brad digests the facts.

"We need t' get Lena," the Asian man states. "Ashara just checked 'er, 'n' she's gettin' worse. If she dies..."

But Floyd isn't listening. The trees before him are deserted, his escape route clear.

I need to go. Got bredren down south who need me. Can't die 'ere savin' da woman dat killed my boy Gurdeep.

So he leaves the lounge and turns towards the front door.

Chapter 53 — Jada Blakowska — 18:05

"Floyd!" *Why's he ignorin' me?* "Floyd! We could really do with some o' those grenades right now!" The Army private's the only survivor to have explosives.

She glances to her right. Luke, who's still staring down the barrel of his rifle, is at the opposite end of the broad kitchen window. "Where the fuck's he gone?"

"Christ knows." Then he gulps, noticeably. "He's not… y' know… fucked off, has he?"

"How would I know? But we need him, now! How many are out there, do you reckon?"

"Dunno. 'Undred? Two 'undred? Fuck knows. There'll be more we can't see, too. Why they movin' so slow, though?"

"The trees seem to slow 'em down. Like water. They're fussier than you'd think, aren't they?"

"Yeah. Gould gone back upstairs?"

She nods. Wrinkles her nostrils. "He grabbed another coupla clips an' went back up. Jesus, that stink is *awful*. Like the water doesn't clean 'em. It makes 'em smell *worse*."

Luke steps back from the window. "I'm gonna go see where Floyd's got to. See if Brad's spotted any t' the rear."

However, Luke is stopped at the kitchen door by Theo, who appears agitated. "Before ya start," the teen begins, "I ain't goin' back upstairs. I ain't a kid. I can 'elp —"

"— Best thing ya can do," Luke says, hands in the air, "is look after yer sister —"

"— No! Fuck that! Where's Floyd?"

"We don't know." Jada deflates. She turns back to the window: the unholy army is getting closer.

"Whaddya mean, ya 'don't know'? Without 'im, we don't stand a chance!"

"'Ang on, Theo," Luke protests. "We survived a day 'n' 'alf without Floyd —"

"— Ya didn't 'ave Lena t' carry, though, did ya? Ya didn't 'ave 'undreds o' them bastards virtually on top o' ya." Theo points at the crowd of zombies outside.

The vanguard are on the driveway. Now, free of the undergrowth, their pace quickens.

"Doors are all locked, right?" Luke's voice was a squeak at first; he clears his throat. "We fire, just keep firin', 'n' we'll make it through this."

"Maybe we should just leave Lena?" Theo's face is white, his forehead damp with sweat.

Luke looks at Jada, eyebrows raised.

"No!" she snaps. "We can't just leave her. That's as good as murder."

"I'm runnin'." Theo leaves the room. "Evie! Get down 'ere, now!"

A shout from Brad halts the footsteps on the stairs. "They're on this side, too!"

Shit. We're surrounded. Our best guy is gone. Can't run. Not enough ammo to fight. Are we gonna die?

When Jada starts to talk, she has the curious feeling that someone else – a stronger, braver version of herself, perhaps – is speaking on her behalf. "Into the basement. Now. All of us."

Luke looks doubtful for a moment. The tap of a transvestite zombie's acrylic nails on the glass spurs him into motion. He slams his window shut.

Jada closes hers. "Gould!" she yells. "Get Ashara an' the kids down here. Brad an' Luke, get Lena." When the children arrive to gape at the growing mob of dead outside, Jada orders them to help her carry as much ammunition and food as possible.

A minute later, the group are at the bottom of the cellar's steep steps, in what can only described as a sex dungeon. Its lights are a darker shade of red. The smell is that of incense mingled with the miasma left behind by the swinger zombies. Toys sit on a rack against one wall; there's some sort of cradle/swing anchored to ceiling and floor. While Connor and Evie stare in confusion, Ashara, Theo and Gabriela share a smirk. The tinkle of breaking windows above sobers the two adolescents in an instant. Footsteps on the floorboards and the crunch of timber come next.

A sweating Luke and Brad lay Lena down on a giant, red-quilted bed. Her flesh is ghostly-pale against the lurid bedding, her body convulsed by shivers.

Thud.

"The basement door!" Gould flourishes his revolver.

"Need to block it!" Jada grabs one end of the dildo cabinet, Luke the other. They haul it up the stairs and wedge it across the threshold. Close behind them is Brad, struggling with a wine cooler. The sex swing jingles as Ashara and Gould detach the apparatus from its hooks; the chain is wrapped around the door handle and secured to the rack.

Thud…. Thud… Thud.. Thud.

We're gonna be slaughtered here, in this perverted place... jeez, I sound like a right prude. But maybe it's weird shit like this, people turnin' away from God, that's caused the apocalypse. Jada shakes her head. *I'm losin' the plot. This shit was caused by Lena an' the likes o' Villeneuve.*

The assault on the door intensifies. No one will ever know the Government's part in the outbreak, because the only evidence, Lena, will die in the next five minutes. She casts around. Now that they've run out of items to stack in front of the door, everything seems to slow down around her.

Luke: grimacing, gaze intent on the pile of furniture, hugging a whimpering Connor to his chest.

Brad: pouring sweat, teeth gritted, his axe cradled like a new-born.

Gould: constantly blinking, hands on hips, lips working.

Theo, Gabriela and Evie: huddled together, heads bowed, shoulders shaking.

Ashara takes Jada's hand. "I'm sorry," the latter says.

"What for?" the shorter, stockier girl asks.

"Bringin' us down here. *Trappin'* us down here."

"What else could we 'ave done? They were all 'round us, weren't they? Anyway, if it weren't fer you, we'd have been killed by those men-in-black, back at the pub."

"I guess." Jada's eyes are filling.

"It's Floyd I blame. He could've saved us. I know we only knew 'im fer a few hours, but he seemed like a good guy. A nice guy. I felt sorry fer 'im when 'is friend died."

"Yeah. I… I suppose I'm shocked, too. But I've hardly thought about it. You just get on with it, don't you?"

"I don't." Ashara flinches as a particularly heavy blow to the door tears a hole in the timber. "I'm always thinkin', all the time, about everythin'. Like even now, talkin', I'm still thinkin' 'bout what it'll be like when they, the zombies… when they're," she lowers her voice and leans in, "gettin' at us. Y' know, *eatin'* us…"

Eatin' us. Jada shudders. "Won't happen." She hefts her assault rifle. I'll save enough bullets for all of us, an' one for myself."

Luke, one arm still around his son's shoulders, looks at Jada with eyes full of meaning. He seems ready to say something.

I like you too, Luke. Shame we couldn't have met under different circumstances.

There's a crunch from the cellar door; a hole has appeared in the timber. Briefly, the hideous visage of a child zomb appears, catching the basement's red light. Immediately, Jada raises her rifle. But the face vanishes, replaced by a dark mass of jostling undead.

"Is this it, Dad?" asks Connor.

"Are we gonna die?" Evie adds.

Boom.

Dust cascades from the ceiling, making most of the survivors cough, sneeze and rub irritated eyes. The explosion doesn't rumble. Its noise, which emanates from the rear of the building – the driveway, perhaps – fades after a couple of seconds, leaving a ringing in Jada's ears.

"The fuck was that?" Brad wonders.

Luke squints at the blockage at the stairs. "Dunno, but there's less o' —"

Three more blasts silence him.

"It's Floyd!" Gabriela says, enthused.

"Knew he wouldn't leave us!" Theo agrees.

Now a gun's firing in sustained bursts. The din is tempered by the concrete ground floor overhead. However, one thing is clear: the machine gun's getting closer. As are footsteps, until they suddenly stop.

Another boom: louder and closer. More dust falls. Earth or stone trickles somewhere above, and there are thuds as larger objects hit the deck. *Bodies, maybe? Has a grenade killed all the zombies thronging the basement door?* The heady scent of jasmine is clouded by that of plaster and stone.

Jada looks at her friends; their expressions have changed from abject terror to hope.

"What if it's them men-in-black, though?" Ashara's back is against the basement's rear wall, as far from the exit as she can be.

Single shots sound.

Footfalls getting nearer. Directly overhead now.

The cellar door handle rattles. A black face materialises at the hole. "Guys? You down dere, guys?"

Yes! Thank fuck for that! Jada's beaming, just like everyone else. Excited chatter bubbles, but Theo's already taking the stairs, two at a time, answering Floyd's question in the affirmative, with Gabriela close behind. The pair are struggling with furniture, so Luke and Brad pitch in. Before long, a soot-dusted Private Nelson is embracing the two adolescents he saved, yesterday, from zombie canines. Laughing along with them like an older brother.

The basement ceiling's still showering grit and powder, so the group rush up the stairs. Lena's carried by Luke and Brad, while Floyd dashes on ahead. The red house has lost all of its eeriness. It's aflame in places, reduced to rubble in others. A couple of singed zombies loiter. They're quickly despatched. Exiting via the front, which is largely unscathed, the survivors find Nelson waiting with a wheelbarrow.

"Put Lena in it." The soldier can't hide his distaste, but he's putting his feelings to one side.

As Luke and Brad place the Evolve CEO in the makeshift stretcher, her blouse is pulled out of place, revealing patches of discoloured skin on her midriff. *Sepsis.* One of Jada's schoolfriends was hospitalised by blood poisoning. Abi Gilliam, who had a similar rash, recovered thanks to a stint in intensive care, a solution currently unavailable to Miss Adderley.

Shit. She can't die. We can't let the Government off the hook. "Come on," she says. Head down, she strides into the woods. She's sweating in the morning sun, and the canopy of dead trees offers respite. Moreover, she can already see concrete. If they can reach the cluster of 1960s tower blocks, they can set up a temporary HQ, leave Lena with the kids and seek medical supplies.

"What the fuck 'appened out there, Floyd?" Luke asks.

"Yeah." Ashara's legs are barely longer than Connor and Evie's, and she's carrying twice the weight, but she's no less verbose than usual. "One minute you're there. Next you've gone."

"Then all those explosions." Theo's not stopped grinning since his hero saved the day.

"Calor gas tanks." Floyd shrugs. "Maybe dey knew somefin' was gonna go down 'n' dey was stockin' up, 'cause dere was loadsa supplies. Anyway, I blew dem up. Da rest was just me with grenades 'n' whatnot."

"How did you know we'd go underground?" asks Joshua Gould. He's the only person still to smile in response to Floyd's exploits.

Great. That's all we need, a schizophrenic gettin' paranoid, causin' shit.

"Seemed like da sensible course o' action. 'N' remember last night, when I said we should bust da basement open? I said den dat it'd be a good place to hole-up."

Brad and Luke must've had doubts of their own, because they watch Floyd's face intently as he answers. They seem content with his explanation, however. Unlike Gould, whose frown deepens.

At the treeline, there's a fence, with a wide gate next to a stile. The closest tower block, a graffiti'd middle finger to the woods and Mother Nature, is less than fifty yards away, across a boggy, yellow field. Apartment buildings two through eight are now visible.

"Come on," says Floyd. "We arc 'round da field. Dat should give us a good view of the space between dis tower 'n' da next one. I go on ahead some 'n' let ya know it's clear. Ya get me?" The soldier does as explained. He ducks behind a bench across a narrow road from the block. He alone has the angle to see past the concrete monolith. After a moment, he rises, shakes his head and mouths the word *zombies*.

Chapter 54 — Randall Maguire — 06:35

Suicide.

Yeah, right. Pull the other one, Villeneuve.

Supposedly, at some point in the early hours, Maguire's boss – no, his predecessor, as of sixty-five minutes ago – smashed an empty brandy decanter against her antique walnut bureau and slashed her own jugular. Part of Agent Maguire wishes he'd been sent to her Belgravia pied a terre, so that he could expose the truth. Of course, had he done so, he would be the next found with a new red smile. Leaving his wife and infant son to fend for themselves.

Disloyalty isn't an option. Nor is failure, as the politician implied on their telephone call an hour ago. When Maguire's helicopter departed London, he wondered if he would ever again set foot in his adopted city.

Barely blinking, he stares out of the chopper window. They're above Stoke-on-Trent now. The outbreak is spreading according to intelligence sources, but it's still to reach this neck of the woods. Fifty miles short of his destination, the agent can't see any of the plumes of smoke currently streaming from Manchester's suburbs. Yet. By the time he arrives on the scene, the western half of the county of Greater Manchester will be wholly or partially compromised.

Success for Maguire does not entail ending the crisis. Not for the time being. The military are responsible for that seemingly insurmountable task. His job, his *only* priority until told otherwise, is to find and eliminate Lena Adderley, thereby severing any credible link between the Government and Evolve plc.

Success for Maguire will not result in medals, commendation or plaudits. Certainly, his promotion to replace Greta Sturridge will accompany an increase in salary. But financial benefits are far from his thoughts. He must succeed because if not, the lives of his nearest and dearest will be forfeit.

Success for Maguire is unlikely. He's searching for a needle in a haystack, the only lead the final communication between Private Floyd Nelson and his superior, Lieutenant Pirie. An approximate last known location probably wouldn't be sufficient for an experienced operative, let alone a jumped-up military liaison officer like Randall Maguire.

He drums his knee with his fingers and tries to ignore the nausea in his empty gut. Still facing the window, he pays no heed to the industrial landscape below; instead, he sees his own reflection: mousy brown hair; boyish good looks giving way to middle age; the stubble from a stressful couple of days. Sniffing, he detects two distinct aromas. His own body odour, worsened by stress, and the black polish on his travelling companion's shiny boots.

"Nervous, sir?" Bloody Barry Jones's voice, heard via headset though the armed man is sat mere feet away, is disarmingly-gentle for a man of his bearing.

Maguire starts nonetheless. "Not as such. More excited, really. Been a while since I was out in the field." There's a confidence in his Irish tones he doesn't feel. "You?"

"Do as I'm told, me, sir."

"But you know what we're facin', right?"

"I've been briefed, sir."

"How in depth did they go, Jones? How much detail?"

"About as in depth as always, sir."

Maguire's forefinger resumes its tattoo on his kneecap. "So they told ya 'bout the nature o' the threat we're facing?"

"Zombies, sir. They're zombies." The subordinate's Welsh lilt upgrades a silly concept to an absurd one. If the younger man is amused by the subject, he doesn't show it. His angular, almost gaunt face remains blank. Flinty eyes betray no emotion whatsoever.

"What did you think, when they told you?"

"*Think*, sir?"

"Yes. What was yer reaction?"

"I went and made ready to deploy, sir."

"Just like that?"

"Just like that. Sir."

"So you didn't have questions?"

"No, sir."

"Ya didn't think to yerself, 'what the fuck, zombies'? Ya didn't wonder how this all came about?" Maguire always becomes more verbose when nervous. Usually, he can control his loose tongue, but usually, he's not twenty minutes from a showdown with the undead.

Jones shifts in his chair. He's tall and lithe, with hard-looking hands. "I know, sir, that they die when they're shot in the head. They showed me a coupla videos, they did."

"But what's yer *opinion* on the whole situation? Stop callin' me 'sir', anyway."

"Okay. To be honest, truth be told, I ain't surprised."

"Yer *not* surprised zombies are runnin' amok?"

"Well, the exact nature o' the problem is a funny one, I'll give you that. The living dead, rising from the grave, eatin' brains!" The hired gun chuckles. "But speakin' more generally, the world's been burnin' fer a while, now. They were warnin' people 'bout global warming, an' all that, years ago. I'm vegetarian m'self. Have been ten years."

Does he know about the chemical, Resurrex? How could he? "But what's climate change got to do with anythin'?"

"Not sayin' it has. Just that *something* was goin' to give at some point. Bit of a shock that the four horsemen of the apocalypse have come in this form to finish us off, but it's as good a way to go as any, I suppose."

"I'd rather be blown up by a nuke or starve to death, to be honest. They eat people alive…"

"I know. I've seen the videos, I 'ave. Pretty gruesome, eh?"

"Yeah. But we just need to focus on our target. Defend ourselves when necessary, yeah, but our priority is Lena Adderley. You've received her profile?"

"Yep." Jones fishes in one of the many pockets in his tactical vest and retrieves a smartphone. "'S all on 'ere."

"Excellent." Maguire falls silent for a while and turns back to the window. He notices the first haze of smoke to the north, but he makes no comment. Instead, in his mind's eye, he sees Caylie, his beautiful wife, playing with Ronan, the bundle of cuteness and energy they struggled for so long to conceive. *I can't fail. I* won't *fail. Whatever I have to do, whatever lengths I have to go to. I'll wipe Manchester off the map if it saves Caylie an' Ronan.*

"Nearly there now, sir."

"We are. Remember. No unnecessary risks. Don't engage with any civilians unless absolutely unavoidable. An' the terrorists —"

"— Sorry, you mean, zombies?"

"Yeah. Of course. Just that every time I've discussed them with anyone, like those numbskulls in the Army, fer example, I've been callin' 'em terrorists."

"That's the official line, isn't it? Terrorists."

Maguire nods. The columns of carbon dioxide are becoming more distinct, now, and he can see specks, like insects, hovering on the horizon. *Drones*. "They are pretty terrifying, after all. Apparently, there are isolated cases poppin' up in other regions. Twelve in London, six in Liverpool, three in Birmingham, two in Bristol, two in Leicester. Single incidents in Newcastle, Glasgow, Huddersfield, Hull. Must be people who were exposed before they travelled. They're bein' contained, though. The only real hotspot is Greater Manchester." He's contracted verbal diarrhoea. Plus he's begun to bounce his heels on the chopper floor, so he makes a conscious effort to slow his breathing.

"Well, don't you worry." Jones shows no sign of anxiety. Were he any more relaxed, he would fall asleep. "I might not look like much, but I've taken on terrorists in the Middle East, in Afghanistan, in Africa, 'ere in the UK, in all kindsa places I wouldn't want to mention 'cause, officially-speakin', I wasn't meant to be there. We'll be home by suppertime, sir. You mark my words."

Maguire smiles tightly. *He better be right, or I'll go the same way as Greta Sturridge. 'Cept she didn't have a spouse an' child to worry about...* A single tear moistens one eye; he swivels hastily in his chair to face the opposite window – away from Jones. *Get a grip, Maguire. Ya knew the risks when ya transferred to Quality Control. Coulda kept yer cushy office at GCHQ, but ya wanted somethin' more 'exciting'. Somethin' 'prestigious' to put on yer CV.* You *knew what ya were gettin' into. What ya were gettin' yer* family *into.*

He needs to stop obsessing about what might happen. Concentrate on matters within his control. Rather than sitting here, fretting, he should be formulating a strategy.

Something in his peripheral vision attracts his attention. It's their escort. An armoured, weaponised unmanned aerial vehicle. Packing more firepower than its diminutive stature – the size of a household gas boiler – might suggest. Reports of an unknown quantity, 'men-in-black' acting outwith Government sanction, have been all-too-common. Satellite and UAV images of the gunmen have shown them using small arms and explosives thus far. Plus, reports of a renegade tank, as fantastic as they sound, need to be taken seriously. Several of the drones have been targetted by rifle fire, so Maguire feels safer with the flying war machine hovering close at hand.

Yer gettin' distracted again.

"So, Jones." He turns towards his muscle. "Let's run over the plan one more time."

The operative opens his eyes. "Sorry, sir, just gettin' some shut-eye, I was. Before I hit the ground."

"No problem. Good idea. I'd have forty winks m'self, but I'm a bit of an insomniac." *Guilty conscience.* "Private Floyd Nelson is our only lead. You've seen his file, yes?"

"I have. Deserter, right?"

"Sort of. But I don't think he'll be the only one, by the time this mess is fixed. There are Army units across Greater Manchester, an' outta the men who survive bein' attacked, a lot don't wanna shoot unarmed civilians on the off-chance they're infected an' ready to turn."

"Some people are squeamish, right enough."

"Luckily, we have coordinates fer his location at a canalside on the border of Mortborough an' Walkley. Unluckily, that was hours ago."

"Likely they'll have moved."

Maguire sighs. "I imagine so." The first fires in the affected zone are now visible: beacons on the horizon warning any sane person to turn around and run. "But we'll have HQ monitoring CCTV, drone and satellite images, so hopefully we can find 'em."

"An' you got me." Jones winks conspiratorially. "I'm a skilled tracker," he elaborates. "They don't call me 'Bloody' 'cause I'm violent. Well, I *am* violent, but the name comes from 'bloodhound'. I'll find this Adderley woman for ya, no worries."

The bravado is delivered so nonchalantly that Maguire can't help but feel reassured. *I've got a simple mission to complete. Find an' eliminate one injured woman. I've got Bloody Jones on my side, as well as the guys at HQ watchin' on TV. I might actually be home by supper —*

A flash in the corner of his eye. Fireball floating in the air, trailing black smoke.

"Takin' evasive action," the pilot tells his passengers via headset. "Hold on, back there."

"What is it?" the Irishman demands. He clutches his belly with one hand as the aircraft loses altitude, while gripping a rubber handle attached to his seat.

"Under fire," the helicopter captain explains.

Jones staggers as he stands but manages to retain his balance. He stoops to peer out of the window on Maguire's side. "Drone's gone. Someone's got surface-to-air missiles."

We're fucked.

Chapter 55 — Naomi Adderley — 06:50

Bump.

The jet lands.

She unbuckles her seatbelt and stands while the wheels are still turning. There are no air stewards to tell her to retake her seat. Apart from the pilot and co-pilot, she's the only person on board. She's at the exit door by the time the aircraft has taxi'd into position, biting at fingernails already chewed to the quick on one hand, holding her overnight bag with the other.

As soon as the hatch opens, Naomi's out into the sunshine, grateful for a break from the recycled cabin air. She enjoys the sun on her face for a moment. Inhales the briny sea air that reminds her of day-trips as a child, when she and her older yet more timid sister, Lena, rode fairground rides and ate fish and chips. Mum, ever the snob, hated Blackpool, so Dad took the girls every school holiday.

There will be no fun or frolics today, however. Not if the news reports broadcasted across the pond are to be believed. *They usually aren't, but I can't take that risk.*

Security's tight. Of course, Naomi crosses passport control without a hitch, but the airport police – armed as heavily as their stateside counterparts – look skittish. Most of their attention is directed at departures, though.

It's her first time at Blackpool International. Manchester is closed, a terrorist strike the culprit according to mainstream media. *Bullshit. They're not completely closing one of the world's largest airports, for over twenty-four hours now, because of one terror attack. Something else is going on.*

It's no coincidence that her sister's incommunicado. Lena never drops off the grid, whether on holiday, locked in conferences or ill. Evolve's new venture is risky; the CEO herself admitted as much during their video chat the previous week, after a couple of glasses of wine.

I should've phoned ahead. Again worrying at her nails, she waits in the car hire queue. While Naomi's not as regimented as her older sibling, it's uncharacteristic of her not to plan in advance, and now she's paying the price. There's no clock ticking. Nothing to suggest she's running out of time apart from the growing unease in her gut. But Naomi's instincts are seldom wrong. At the moment, they're screaming a warning.

For the dozenth time, she looks out of the large, ceiling-to-floor windows. Abnormal police presence and slightly 'off' atmosphere aside, all seems well. The car park is quiet, but the hour is early. She yawns; her sleep on the overnight flight from LAX was fitful.

She's just taken the keys for an anonymous Audi saloon and is halfway across the parking lot when her phone buzzes in her jeans back pocket. She checks the cracked screen she should've repaired after last week's sporting expedition. *Panucci. About fucking time, you lazy bastard.* "Hello?"

"Naomi? You called?" The grandson of Neapolitan immigrants, Giuseppe Cesare Panucci has a faintly Mancunian accent. He sounds flustered.

"Yes. Three hours ago."

"Sorry. Been kinda busy."

"Why, what's wrong? You haven't been busy since you left uni, and you weren't particularly busy there."

"Ha ha. We're leavin' town. Me, Mama, Papa, the old folks. Goin' to Wales. We're leavin' in a minute."

"But why?" Spotting her allocated vehicle amongst the pool of MotoHire rentals, Naomi points the key fob and unlocks the doors. "What's going on? Surely it's not this terrorist —"

"— The terrorist thing is BS, Naomi." Someone nearby raises their voice. Panucci replies with a stream of Italian. "There are no *terrorists* —"

"— So what is it, then? And why are the media saying different? What's going on?"

"I'd tell you, but you'd only laugh."

"Just spit it out, Panucci. You know me better than that."

"It's… it's…"

"What?" She opens the navy blue car's driver passenger side door, then remembers the steering wheel's on the right-hand side. "What is it?"

"Zombies." There's a shuffling, the packing of bags, perhaps.

"What?"

"Fuckin' zombies, Naomi. The undead. People dyin' an' comin' back to life!"

"Panucci… you're being ridiculous. What the fuck are you talking about?"

So he tells her. Much of Greater Manchester overrun by the walking dead. Army battling zombies on the streets. Families torn apart. Press blackout. Rumours spread by a select few escapees…

She takes a moment. Wrinkles her nose at the pungent 'cotton candy' scent of the air freshener, starts the car, connects her phone to the Bluetooth, checks her reflection in the mirror – her pixie-style hair could use some attention – then asks if he's still on the line.

"Yeah." His voice is more distant now; he's on speakerphone. An engine starts, and tyres screech.

"Have you actually seen any of these… zombies yourself?"

"No. They haven't reached Wilmsley yet. An' I don't plan to. There 'aven't been any cases reported in Wales, yet."

"Okay. Could they not be…" *You're not going to persuade him he's wrong, Naomi. Just let him do what he needs to do.* "Forget it. When are you leaving?"

"We're already movin'. Papa's drivin' the old minibus. Hopefully we'll get away in time. Roads are being cordoned off everywhere… it's mayhem. Just be glad you're in the States."

"But I'm not. I'm in England. Blackpool. I —"

"— Shit, Naomi! You've made a big mistake."

"I *had* to come! Lena's ghosting me. I'm scared she's… involved in all this."

"Why would she be?"

"I… I'm not sure…"

"'Ang on a minute." His voice lowers. "Lena's company… they're into fertilisers, agriculture, all that shit. Right?"

"Yeah."

"So let's not play dumb, Nai. I've seen the planes in the last coupla days, spewin' chemicals everywhere. Shitloads of 'em. They're tryin' to dose people up, aren't they? To protect us from whatever shit your sister's unleashed."

The thought had occurred to me, yes. "I don't know, Pepe. Honestly. What you're saying makes sense, though." As she slips into first gear and drives towards the car park exit, Naomi checks the skies for chem-dumping aircraft. *You idiot. You're at an airport, so you're bound to see airplanes.* "I'm worried sick, though. I need to find Lena."

"Okay. Well, I'm gonna be on the road for the next few hours. Probably all day judgin' by this traffic. But I've got my phone on me, my laptop. I'll do what I can to help. Put the feelers out."

"You've still got all your old contacts from… you know…"

"I do. Some of 'em owe me favours, too."

"Great. It's just that I might need pretty drastic measures…"

Panucci expels air through his nostrils. "I was hoping you wouldn't say that."

Naomi turns onto an A-road, heading for the closest motorway. "Hardware, Pepe. If I'll be coming across the sort of things you've mentioned —"

"— Then you run. You don't fight these things. If trained solders an' machine gun drones can't beat 'em, you can't either. I don't care how many huntin' trips an' war games you've been playin'. Mortborough, where your sister's based, is ground zero accordin' to the rumours. Streets full o' the walkin' dead. The stories I've heard about those things…"

"Okay, okay. I get the message. But I *am* going to look for Lena. I'll do my best to steer clear of these… zombie-things, but if I do come across them in the wild, I want to be prepared."

"Right. I'll do my best, an' I'll call you back. Probably tomorrow, it'll be."

"No! Sorry, Pep, but that's no good. If things are as bad as you say, Lena's in real danger. Not just from the 'zombies', but…" *Should I mention my suspicions about the Government people she's been dealing with?*

"Say no more. I think I get the gist." Panucci clicks his tongue; in the background, there's hushed chatter in Italian. "Listen. I'll do my very best to track down Lena. You head to Manchester in the meantime, an' I'll bell you when I know something."

"And the hardware?"

"I'll get on it straightaway. An' Nai?"

"Yeah?"

"My time, that's yours gratis, but the hardware…"

"I'll see you right, Pepe. Bye."

"Take care."

She will pay him handsomely, of course. Naomi owns her own cosmetic company based in Los Angeles, and her family is fabulously rich. Besides, she would bankrupt herself if doing so was necessary to save her sister. Driving past the landmark windmill on the outskirts of Blackpool, she has a vivid flashback that brings a tear to her eye. Dad driving the Range Rover. Her and Lena in the back, fighting over a £5 illuminated toy bought at The Illuminations. They used to argue frequently. But they would play more often.

I'll find her and protect her, whatever it takes. Just like I always did. Shame I've not been around recently to keep an eye on her. I'll make up for it, though.

Onto the M55 Naomi drives. No faster than 75mp/h, for she doesn't want to get stopped by police. There are plenty of them on the road, too, their lights flashing cold blue. *Something isn't right.*

Obviously, it's nothing to do with creatures from beyond the grave. Giuseppe Panucci's an intelligent man, who's used his talents for ill-gotten gains without once falling foul of the long arm of the law. He has a vivid imagination, however, and he can be suggestible. There will be a logical explanation for the recent unrest.

Traffic is heavy where the highway meets the M6. Naomi switches on the radio, hoping to hear travel news. The usual bland pop plays no matter which station she selects, so she finds Classic FM and allows the soothing melodies to ease her mind.

Once she's joined the nation's longest motorway, the congestion lessens. Or it does at first. She spots tailbacks in the distance, the smoke of a vehicle fire, perhaps. Emergency responders are utilising the hard shoulder, as are a number of motorists willing to bend the rules to reach their destination more quickly. Eventually, even that lane is at a standstill.

Typical. Another quarter of a mile away, there's an exit for a service station and the local area. If she'd got there a couple of minutes earlier, she could've turned off and found a diversionary route. *The A6, maybe. That's near here, and it goes to Manchester as well.*

She huffs, glances at her rear-view mirror. The line of traffic is lengthening. Above them, the sky is brightening, the haze clearing. An aeroplane, not quite as large as an airliner and painted dark green, flies over. It spews a stream of white smoke. *Is what Pep said really true? If it is, and there's some kind of dangerous chemical in the air, I could get ill just by being here.* "Come on!" She bangs the steering wheel with both hands.

A crunch of metal, somewhere up ahead, grabs her attention. She cranes her neck to look past the cars ahead but sees nothing of note. She could get out of the Audi. Maybe go and chat to some of the other motorists who've tired of waiting. Something's itching at the back of her mind, however. It's intuition, a primal aversion to moving, to making herself visible and vulnerable. Or is she simply unnerved by Panucci's lurid horror-story?

Then there's a scream.

Naomi covers her mouth. Perversely, now she *does* want to get out and investigate. Hand shaking, she opens her door by a crack, but as she does, she spots a flash of movement in the driver side wing-mirror. Instantly, she pulls the handle shut, closes her window, wriggles down in her seat. *I really should've rung Panucci* before *leaving the States. Arranged for his hardware guy to meet me on arrival.*

More screams.

Terrorists. The official line is terrorists are causing the emergency, but if that's the case, why are there no gunshots; why no bombs? And why would anyone, however motivated, commit an act of terror on the M6 motorway?

A strange bumping sound is getting closer, and it's coming from behind Naomi. Bump, scrape, bump, with an occasional crack of glass, punctuated by yells of fright.

Need to see what's going on.

Slowly, she inches up her seat, until she can see the road once more. One of the drivers that exited their vehicle, a man roughly fifty years of age, is pointing straight at Naomi. He breaks into a run whilst looking over his shoulder. Even from twenty yards' distance, the dread in his expression is obvious.

Bump, right over her head this time. Lips pursed, she sits rigidly, like a field mouse beneath an owl.

Scrape, crack. The saloon's windscreen spiderwebs under a Doc Marten boot. A dark-clothed humanoid leaps onto the white Mini in front and continues its journey.

Middle-aged man is sprinting by this point, as are other onlookers. They're turning off the highway, into a roadside field. Suddenly, the dark figure, who's drawing level with the escapees, jumps to the left off a hatchback rather than proceeding forwards. The bottom half of its body vanishes as it ploughs through the yellow grass.

At the back of the fleeing pack stumbles a young boy. Red-faced, ginger-haired, he wears a neck brace. He's carrying a single grey crutch. When he turns he swings the support and hits the pursuing ghoul on its bearded chin. The thing freezes. For a single, giddy moment, Naomi thinks the hunter has been pacified. And then it pounces and brings the child down.

Shit.

Now there are more of the freaks. Some scramble across and between gridlocked cars to chase the runners; others are attacking the vehicles themselves.

Steeling herself, Naomi slips out the door and runs for the field.

Chapter 56 — Randall Maguire — 07:20

The Little Weston supermarket car park is all but deserted. Jones has recce'd the immediate area outside, finding nothing of note. So it's time to get out. Randall's simultaneously relieved and afraid; he'd begun to feel claustrophobic in the bullet-ridden helicopter, and he needs to begin his mission post-haste, but he's also scared. With good reason, too.

Threat one: although the chopper didn't get shot down like its escort drone, it wasn't for the lack of trying. A missile, launched their way, missed by a hair's breadth. Machine-gun fire injured the pilot, Briggs. She was forced to land prematurely, and if she doesn't receive medical attention soon she'll die. Clearly, an unidentified third party with serious firepower objects to Maguire's presence. Venturing out of their transport could easily take them into the crosshairs of said mystery assailants.

Like Maguire, Briggs knew the risks involved when she joined the department, so, barring a miracle, she'll bleed out. The collar bone wound she incurred has been patched up, but she needs a hospital. In any event, the stricken woman may not be afforded the luxury of exsanguination. Because there's a threat two. During their rushed descent, Maguire got his first glimpse of the monsters. The shambling, rotting freaks whose existence he could never quite acknowledge. The dirty secret he has to protect. The B-movie extras, smeared with blood and filth. The undead.

Focus, Maguire. He's staring at Jones, who's hunkered behind a grimy estate car, his assault rifle pointing up. The smell of burnt plastic almost masks something fouler. The sky is baby-blue, the clouds mere wisps. Already, there's a balmy feel in the air. It's going to be another beautiful day.

Should I say something to Briggs? The pilot's a sorry sight, her skin milky-white, her bobbed blonde hair speckled red. Maguire pities her, but what could he say that might alleviate her suffering? Meaningless platitudes and promises? She's a professional; she would rather be treated as one.

After a final glance left and right – there's a high wall to their rear – the agent jumps to the ground and scampers over to the Welshman.

"You good, sir?" The urban-camouflaged paramilitary gives him the briefest of glances.

"Yeah," Maguire lies. He draws his pistol, a Glock 17, from a shoulder holster on the inside of his suit jacket. In his other hand is a mobile telephone. The maps app shows him and his minder as a blue dot, with Private Nelson's last known location a red pin. "We're about a mile away from the pub where Nelson buzzed Pirie. See."

Briefly, Jones looks away from the sprawling supermarket. "Yeah. Seems like mostly fields, to me."

"Which suits us, accordin' to the experts. The zombies mainly stick to built-up areas, suburbs. Not semi-rural."

"That won't apply to our rocket-launchin', drone-blastin' friends in black, though, will it?"

"No, I guess not."

"Come on, then. Why don't you cover while I dash across the car park? Sir."

"Of course." Maguire watches, gun in hand, as his man makes his way across the tarmac.

Then the favour is returned. They're both stood outside the shop, a smokers' shelter the only thing stopping anything in the supermarket from seeing them. Nevertheless, his skin crawls. *Those men-in-black could have eyes on us right now. Probably wouldn't even hear the shot. Bullet in the head. Dead 'fore I know it.*

Which is presumably why Jones is using his rifle scope to check the roofs of nearby houses. "If I see so much as a peep from them bastards in black, I'll stick their fuckin' rocket launcher up their arse."

Despite the other man's bluster, Maguire feels uneasy about their mysterious foes. "Nelson mentioned 'em, apparently. The MIBs. He presumed they were allies, some special forces branch. He even offered to take Adderley to 'em!"

"Jesus." Jones skirts the smoking shelter, bolts across the supermarket forecourt, past cash machines and a trolley park, and stops at the far corner of the building. He covers as his superior catches up. "Good job he didn't, isn't it?"

"Very good job." Maguire breathes shallowly. He's a little out of shape, but he doesn't want his super-fit comrade to know. "Woulda been *very* embarrassing. Whole shit-show could *still* be very embarrassing. But this is our opportunity to sort it out. We find Nelson. We use him to find Adderley." *If we survive long enough.*

"So that's the priority?" Jones raises a hand to keep Maguire back while he peeks around the corner. He takes a cursory look, then uses his scope to scrutinise more carefully. "The Adderley woman?"

"Yeah. Course, if we can gather intel on these MIBs, that'd be great too."

"So… the whole 'zombie' deal… that's *not* the priority?"

He's got a point. One o' Europe's most populous conurbations has descended into hell, an' we're focussed on coverin' our arses. "Yeah… I see where yer comin' from…" A faraway boom, a tank or artillery piece firing, perhaps, saves his graces. "The zombies are *their* priority. Regular Army. Once they get a grip of the situation, everythin'll be okay."

"Hmm." The paramilitary beckons and points; Maguire joins him at the building's corner. "Everythin' won't be okay for that poor bugger, will it, sir?"

The agent swallows. He tries to avert his eyes, but they linger on the crow's blood-sheened beak excavating a young girl's eye socket. The bird returns his glare. Its head is cocked to one side. An eyeball dangles from its mouth. Hearing muffled, vision tinted red, Maguire manages to turn away. Although he stares down the road leading into Little Weston centre, he barely registers its surgeries, salons and shops.

"Come on. Across the street, to that bus shelter. We stop there, then into that park. Keep yer head down. Sir."

Broadley Park is empty. It's full of dry trees yet devoid of living people. There are plenty of dead ones, though. They lie on yellow grass; they're slumped across benches and water features; they're focal points for birds and scavenging mammals. Thankfully, none are moving. A couple of dogs regard the living humans with wariness, but the animals keep their distance.

Maguire has to make a conscious effort to maintain walking pace, as though the sickening set-pieces he passes emit some sort of psychic sludge. "This is…" He pauses for so long that he almost forgets he was speaking. "Fuckin' grim. I've seen the videos, but they don't do it justice. An' the smell… it's…" Indescribable, so Maguire doesn't even try.

"It is that. Very grim." Jones's sharp cheekbones have slumped in his face; his eyes are listless. "I mean, I've seen some shit in my time. But there's a difference between soldiers wi' bullet wounds an'… this."

The Welshman's right. Most of the fallen have been feasted upon, first by their murderers, and then by carrion-birds, animals and insects.

"Shit," says Maguire, suddenly jolted from his torpor. In fifty yards, where the dead trees are less dense, their route will take them alongside a playground, in which there are half a dozen individuals. He draws his pistol. "They're so still."

"That's why we didn't see 'em till now. But don't worry, sir." Jones drops to one knee, raises his rifle.

"Shouldn't we just go around 'em? There's gotta be another way. Firin' might attract more —"

Suddenly, his point is rendered moot. Like puppets simultaneously possessed by some insidious force, they jerk into motion. They're deceptively-swift, too, with the fastest goose-stepping out of the yard and onto the main pathway in a couple of seconds. Wearing the all-green of a paramedic, it still carries a defibrillator in one hand. Its tunic is shredded and stained dark.

The male zombie's head explodes as Jones's gun spits lead. Immediately, the shooter adjusts his aim to land an identical shot on the female teenager close behind. Numbers three and four go down with the same efficiency.

Maguire is transfixed. He's never seen rounds fired in a live environment; thus far, most of his career has been in counter-intelligence, stopping threats before they develop. Now he's watching walking dead people being executed in a quiet Manchester park.

A thud to his rear has him spinning on his heel. Five paces away, a zombie boy has materialised. "Jones!"

Unflustered, the Welshman turns and pulls the trigger. His slug takes the ragged urchin mid-leap, bringing it to the ground a couple of yards short of Maguire. Another infant, this one a girl barely four years old, falls from the trees. It receives a bullet in the mouth before it can regain its footing.

Playground zombie five has now gained ground, however. Arms reaching out, the rotund male takes small but rapid steps, its gashed head shaking from side to side as if in firm disagreement. Six is more listless. The twenty-something female has one leg tangled in the climbing frame.

Jones slays the fat man without ceremony. "You wanna take the last one?" he asks, staring into the branches above.

"Okay." Maguire chambers a round in his gun, realising he should've done so as soon as the first zombie came into view. With his aide close behind, he stalks the final foe. Even within thirty feet, the once-attractive ginger haired beast makes no attempt to attack. Teeth gritted, Maguire levels his handgun, aiming between green eyes. *Headshot. Needs to be a headshot.*

His finger tenses on the trigger for an age. Yet he can't pull. *It's… defenceless.*

Suddenly, the creature is alive, spitting and writhing to free itself from the jungle gym. Maguire blows its brains out, then dry-retches.

"You might have to be quicker than that next time, sir," Jones says lightly.

The park is just a few hundred yards wide, but the journey from one side to the other seems never-ending. Happily, there's another road beyond, and fields after that, so they should get a break from the corpses.

Vehicles are more commonplace on Sullivan Drive. Some are parked roadside; others are positioned haphazardly, in the middle of the thoroughfare.

"Think we're clear o' Little Weston, now," Jones says, his gaze flitting from building to car, hedgerow to lamp-post as they cross the street.

"Thank fuck fer that." Maguire has eyes only for the open acres ahead. Trees are within a hundred paces, their limbs too bare to hide zombie climbers or snipers. With a moderate breeze, and the sunrays strengthening, the hike is almost pleasant. If he doesn't think about dead flesh covered in flies. Or dead arms and legs twitching and convulsing. Or dead skulls impacted by high-velocity rifle rounds. Or dead redheads, stinking of faeces and vomit, eyes like ice, jaws slack and wide... *Stop it, Randall. Yer losin' it,*

They cross a fence into a farmer's field, where the brown grass has been chewed to the soil. A herd of almost-skeletal cattle, huddled together in their misery, become alert as soon as Maguire and Jones step foot on their pasture.

"Is it just me," the former begins, his pace slowing, "or do those cows look like they want to eat us?"

"Don't be daft!" Jones grins. "Sir. Sorry. But they're herbivores, they are. Don't eat meat, do they?"

"No. Yer right. But… should they be… walking toward us like that?"

"Dunno, sir. They do look a bit… cross, though, don't they? I'm the last person they should be goin' for, though! I haven't eaten steak fer years!"

Maguire smiles dutifully, but he can't shake off the unease. Several tons of livestock is headed their way. "Are they bulls, maybe? Are we on their territory, or somethin'?"

"You wouldn't get that many bulls together, I don't think. Shit." Jones stops, looks left and right for an alternative route.

The ground beneath their feet begins to rumble. Maguire blinks, but his eyes aren't deceiving him: the cows are now charging, and they're faster than they look.

Chapter 57 — Floyd Nelson — 08:00

Two hostiles. One male adult: six feet tall; muscular build; Asian; wearing vest, short, flip-flops One female adult: five feet six inches tall; slim build; Caucasian; wearing tracksuit. *Stood dere nexta dat burnt Merc, doin' fuck all. No threat.*

One hostile: male adolescent; moving quickly across the car park. *Take him out.*

The high-powered round enters the back of the target's head, an inch below a skullcap clipped to curly black hair. The gore-smeared slug leaves the cranium between the eyebrows, before expending its kinetic force on concrete. Dark crimson squirts from the entry wound. Brain matter, skull and blood spews from the other side. The zombie's legs lose power. Face first it falls, mashing the remainder of its cannibalised nose on the car park kerb.

Hurry up! Floyd takes a brief break from over-watch to track his friends' progress. *Fuck, dey slow.*

Upon arrival at Churchill Heights, the apartment complex closest to the woods, the group found the surrounding area – its car park, a row of three shops, a pitiful playground – to be haunted by the undead. Not infested per se, but with more than enough monsters to turn a bad day into a terrible one.

Plus, a hurried check revealed every entrance to the tower block to be locked or blocked. Entering the next high-rise, Chamberlain Heights, was mooted, until zombies were spotted through its windows.

A decision had to be made, and quickly, for the dead who survived Floyd's improvised tactical strike were sure to catch up soon.

Therefore, the weary, harried survivors decided to climb to a first floor balcony, where an open French window would allow them into the flats. Using equipment found in a tree surgeon's abandoned van, in the car park, they're ascending. One at a time. Luke went first. Then Brad. The harness was passed down and secured to a still-unconscious Lena, and she was hauled to safety. Evie and Connor received the same treatment. Theo and Gabriela managed the feat without help. Ashara tried, failed, and was eventually lifted by the others.

Meanwhile, Floyd's been sniping any zombies aiming to prevent their escape. He's amidst the upper branches a mighty oak, one of the forest's outlying trees. Two hundred metres from the courtyard. And, in fairness, he's enjoying himself. *Man should take pride in his work, ya get me?* Would he revel in the endeavour as much if he were aiming at actual living people?

It's not the right time for introspection, though. He needs to concentrate for another ten minutes or so, and then he can rejoin the gang.

Gould's slowing the process: the bus station supervisor, who complained of an injured shoulder before bed last night, is insisting on attempting the rope climb alone, while the others remonstrate.

Come on, fool. Just let dem 'elp ya. You ain't less of a man 'cause ya need 'elp.

Of those present, Jada, despite being the only other person yet to reach safety, shows the most patience. *She a good gal, dat one.*

Shit! He's been focussing on the squabbling humans too much. Four zombies are scrambling towards the man and woman at the bottom of the rope. Luke, leaning over the balcony rail, points in alarm.

Eye to the scope, Floyd sights the fastest. His shoulder bucks as he looses the first bullet. No time for headshots, so it's the fiend's right thigh that takes the lead. Down the lanky male goes, only to immediately start crawling. *Finish 'im off in a min.*

Shot two shatters the hip of a sprinting teenaged girl. It spins, raven hair swirling, and slumps to the ground.

Shot three misses an elderly gent by a whisker; four blows a hole through its chocolate-skinned neck.

One left. Limping due to a half-eaten left calf, the shorts-wearing middle-aged man is within ten paces of Jada and Josh Gould. She turns, assault rifle at the ready. Two bangs equal two red flowers blossoming in the crisp white of the zomb's shirt.

Nice one, gal. Floyd executes the two freaks he disabled, wipes sweat from his brow, adjusts his position in the tree, winces at a splinter in his thumb.

And it comes from nowhere.

From under one of the burnt-out cars used as a door barricade, in fact, as if it's been unconscious or only just turned. It can't weigh more than eight stone, but the mini-skirted office worker moves with the fury and speed of a puma.

Floyd's forefinger squeezes his trigger, with no effect. *Shit. Outta ammo.* Mechanically, he reloads while squinting into the distance.

Gould's almost up to the first floor and is powerless to react. When Jada raises her rifle, nothing happens.

She outta ammo too.

From above, Luke and Brad can't get the right angle to assist, either.

Two figures have become one; the undead attacker's upon Jada now. Up comes Floyd's rifle, the scope into his line of sight, air into his lungs. Jada's holding her own, gripping the beast by its throat, while it grasps at her face. Like partners in a bizarre dance, except one is screaming for her life.

Releasing half a breath, Private Nelson fires once. He had to aim low, to the right, or risk the bullet striking his fellow survivor once it's torn through the enemy. The zombie sags. Its ankle's a mess of blood, bone and tendon.

Meaning Jada can shove her assailant to the ground and reel away. She grabs the rope Gould's relinquished and drags herself upwards.

Another blast from Floyd's gun dispatches the dead cannibal as it rises to one knee. Inhaling through his nose, exhaling between gritted teeth, the soldier scans the courtyard for new threats. His scrutiny falls on the pair he dismissed moments ago, who are making a move for towards the dancing rope as it dangles beneath Jada. *Not so fast, freaks.* He makes craters in both of their heads and sniffs. *Time to go.*

They've taken too long, however. Floyd's been so bent on saving his friends that he's not noticed the undead from the canal and the woods. Some are bloated from their watery graves, others singed by the fires that consumed the red house. They're streaming towards Churchill Heights, with many passing directly underneath the marksman on his perch. The putrid cocktail of varying degrees of decomposition assaults his nostrils. Somehow, the crowd haven't spotted Private Nelson in his eyrie, but they surely will if he descends.

Fuck. Dat prick Gould to blame for dis. Fuckin' about. Now I's stuck 'ere, in dis tree. Until dose ugly bastards find me.

He could wait it out, let the horde by, then sneak past them and into the flats. Not the greatest of plans, admittedly, but what alternative does he have? He laments opting not to take one of the radios. They were malfunctioning earlier; he was too impatient to wait for them to be fixed. One of his comrades might now contrive a better way for him to reunite with the group, and Floyd will be none the wiser.

Shit.

Growing uncomfortable, he shifts his bulk and waits for a gap in the dead procession. The cramp in his leg isn't abated, but he gets another splinter for his trouble.

A thud from below, on the other side of the oak, has his heart rate thundering. Reflexively, he twists to investigate: a particularly tall and portly zombie has blundered into the tree. Of course, the timber absorbs the impact, but Private Nelson's sudden movement in response causes a twig to snap.

A dead child's straw-coloured bangs bounce, its head jerking back as though caught on a fisherman's line. Cold blue eyes meet Floyd's own. For the briefest of moments, there's something in the shared moment. Emotion, empathy almost. Then the shark-stare returns. The girl leaps at the tree trunk, only to bounce off. Then try again. And fall away once more.

The zombette's too short to reach the lowest branch, but some of its peers are becoming interested. *Shit. Shit, shit, shit. Can't shoot dem all.* He peers through his rifle scope at the Churchill Heights first floor balcony, where Jada and Luke are using their own telescopic sights to look his way. He sees concern on their faces. Although they'll help if they can, they don't have enough ammunition or the long range shooting skill to kill the dozens of undead now thronging the solitary oak.

Is dis it? Have I given my own life to save deirs?

He's pouring with sweat now, feeling nauseous. Bile in his mouth. Glancing down only worsens the fear, for two of the zombies – both young men, one caramel-skinned, the other Caucasian – are making progress. Their blackening fingers find notches and cracks in tree bark. Their haste works against them, as do the grasping hands of their fellow zombs. Several times they fall, yet they're undeterred. Meanwhile, others are beginning their own ascents.

Soon, there are five monsters clinging to the wood, getting higher. Closer to their prey. Eyes crazed, eyes vacant, eyes bloodshot, eyes glacial. Mouths agape, teeth bared, the blood of other victims encrusted in beards and fringes.

Lips curled into a sneer, Floyd can't remain idle any longer. He swings his rifle, points downwards and puts a hole in the forehead of the most agile climber, while the second quickest takes a slug between the eyes. Gore showers those below. The gun's noise attracts even more of the enemy, though. The double-dead men are promptly replaced.

Over the next couple of minutes, Floyd blasts another half-dozen predators. He has several spare magazines, but he doesn't have enough ammunition to kill every zombie. Perhaps sensing his predicament, Luke, Jada and Brad lend their own fire. No doubt anxious of hitting their friend by accident, they aim for the press at the base of the tree trunk rather than those already on their way up.

Still the dead come.

And the supporting fire from Churchill Heights is ebbing away.

The crackle of assault rifles is replaced, however, by that of heavier gunfire, as though someone's found a heavy machine gun in the tower. Now the zombies beneath Floyd are being scourged rather than withered. They fall to the ground gushing blood, with ragged bullet holes, cratered crania and severed appendages. Huge wooden daggers are ripped from the tree and embed themselves in corrupting flesh. One sliver pierces Floyd's right forearm; he gasps and hugs the tree limb more tightly. The din is chastening, the smell of blood and guts worse.

Frowning, the saved soldier peers through his scope at his friends. Luke and Jada are pointing, frantically jabbing at the air with their forefinger. Floyd looks up and realises why.

A drone, larger than usual, hovers no more than thirty yards away. The cannon under its nose is aflame as it sprays shells at the mass of inhumanity. Meanwhile, any zombies coming from the woods are picked off by a secondary weapon, a longer-barrelled gun that judders each time it discharges. Within half a minute, every monster is down. The ground around the oak is drenched dark, littered with bodies and timber shavings.

Floyd looks at the UAV.

Whirring, the machine refocuses on the man it saved.

Chapter 58 — Luke Norman — 08:10

"We need t' shoot it down!" He rests his assault rifle on the balcony railings. It's a long shot, and if he misses, he could hit Floyd.

Brad puts a hand on the gun's barrel and flinches at the heat. "Ya forgettin' what 'appened last time we shot down a drone?"

Luke blinks, confused. Then he remembers: the battle on the chemical plant roof, yesterday. When an all-out assault on a military UAV led to a surgical missile strike. They narrowly-escaped with their lives, but there's no guarantee they'll be as lucky today. *'N' we've got the kids with us now. Can't risk 'em nukin' the tower block. If only it were that simple.* "We can't just let 'im die, though!"

Jada's using her own ACOG sight. "Floyd… he's hidin' his face, isn't he? See."

She's right. The drone suddenly elevates, making the observers start.

"Is it tryin' t' get a better look?" Luke wipes sweat from his eyes then squints through his sight once more.

"Dunno." Brad puffs his cheeks. "It ain't lightin' 'im up, anyway. That's the weirdest thing. Why's it not just shootin' 'im, like it did with all the zombs?"

"Not shootin' 'im *yet*." Luke licks his lips. "It could open fire any minute, 'n' we'll have just let 'im die. After he saved us at the pub, 'n' at the red 'ouse. Plus he 'elped us all get in 'ere safely. We can't just let 'im die, fer fucksake!"

"Perhaps it… recognises him." Jada clicks her tongue. "They're Army drones, right? An' he's deserted from the Army. Maybe that's why it's not firin'."

"He said one fired on 'im 'n' his buddy, Gurdeep," Brad says. "In some industrial estate in Swinford, or somethin'."

Whatever. We're still just stood 'ere, watchin', 'n' it could blow 'is guts all over that fuckin' tree at any moment. "We 'ave t' do somethin'."

The door behind them opens; it's Gould. "What are you all doing?" The bus station supervisor throws his hands in the air. "You need to get inside! That's not the only drone, remember."

Theo's head appears at the window. "What's goin' on?"

"Nothin', just stay inside," says Luke. He rubs the back of his neck. Jada and Brad are simply looking at each other, frozen in indecision. Lack of rest and excess stress are taking a toll on all of them.

Fuck it. Need t' do somethin'.

The others merely gape as Luke raises his rifle and fires in one smooth motion. At such a range, with his limited expertise, it's a difficult shot, and his attempt flies high and wide.

"What the fuck, Luke?" Jada and Brad say in synchrony.

Gould unleashes a barrage of expletives and heads back inside, ushering Theo and Gabriela in the process.

Luke fires again. "We just need t' distract it! Not blow it up."

Jada nods. "If we can just get it to look this way, we'll give Floyd the chance to escape." She aims and shoots a single round.

"Fuck it." Brad shrugs. "Don't reckon we could destroy it from 'ere anyway. Not wi' the ammo we've got left." His effort is the most accurate, but it's also too close to Private Nelson.

Slowly, deliberately, the hunter/killer spins one hundred and eighty degrees.

"Down!" Jada yells.

All three duck. They can see through the railings; hopefully, the drone cannot. It pauses for a moment, hovering.

Can't give away our position. If we do, we could 'ave a dozen o' those metal bastards 'ere, blastin' us t' fuck. Moving slowly, Luke manoeuvres himself and his rifle in order to use the sight. "He's almost down from the tree!"

The other two take a look for themselves. "Go on, Floyd, leg it!" Brad whispers.

As if he can hear them, the infantryman hits the ground and sprints towards a patch of wasteland.

"Quick!" Jada says.

Floyd's heading for a burnt-out vehicle. He'll be too slow, though, for the cover is ten yards away, and the drone's turning again.

Bang.

"Brad!" Jada hisses. "You'll give us away."

"It worked, though, eh?" Luke says.

They've got the UAV in a quandary. Its controller knows Floyd is somewhere nearby, but the rifle fire's the bigger threat.

"He's safe!" Brad points.

Their comrade has dived and rolled under the old estate car.

"Thank fuck Salton's such a shithole," says Luke.

Brad laughs. "Yeah. Burnt-out cars are nothin' new 'round 'ere."

"Now he's stuck, though." Jada huffs.

"So we fire some more shots." Brad aims again.

"Use pistols, then," Jada suggests. "Better than wastin' all our good ammo."

"Too long range," Luke argues.

"Nah." Brad has a sidearm tucked into his belt, so he draws it. "Reckon it's the *sound* that's buggin' it." He looses a round at the UAV, which floats about thirty feet above ground, roughly thirty yards from Floyd's hiding spot. It's still facing the massive oak tree.

Sure enough, the machine reacts.

"See!" says Brad, shooting once more.

"Fair dues." Luke slides open the apartment's door. It's gloomy inside, but he knows where the weapons are. When his son and the others, seated around a kitchen-dinner table, look at him expectantly, he promises to explain all soon.

One of the pistols stolen from the MIBs is on a nest of tables next to the sofa. Another shot is fired outside as he stoops to collect the gun. Covered in blankets and lying on the couch, Lena stirs and whimpers, giving Luke a start.

Back on the balcony, he, Brad and Jada alternate in taking pot-shots at the drone. Only the latter is successful, her third try scratching the machine's paintwork. It'd already begun to drift their way anyway, but the on-target effort hastens its flight. The three snipers duck.

Brad watches the wasteland through his rifle scope. "Keep firin'," he says. "Floyd's comin' outta hidin'. 'Ang on. He's wavin' at us. Tellin' us t' stop, I think. Pointin'..."

The whirr of a second hunter/killer over their heads has them all flat on their bellies.

"Floyd's still tellin' us t' stop. Now *he's* hidin' again... the drone near 'im is turnin' 'round again... 'n' we're back at square one."

"'Cept that now we got *two* o' the fuckers to content with." *Fuck.* Luke turns onto his back to risk a skywards glance. The new UAV is almost directly over their heads. Although most of its body is concealed by the balconies above them, the under-nose cannon protrudes.

"We could do wi' gettin' back inside." Brad begins to crawl. A buzz in the sky stops him in his tracks. "It's movin'!"

"Just freeze!" Jada hisses. "If we're completely still, it might not notice us."

So they lie motionless, praying. Uncomfortable on the concrete of the balcony, sweating. Luke's world has shrunken with his perspective. Belly-down, facing out into the open air, pigeon faeces inches from his face on the floor, he can see little of note. He smells rotten flesh on the breeze, but the tang of his fellow humans' unwashed bodies is stronger. Time slows to a standstill as he waits for their luck to change.

Warm fingers, Jada's, intertwine with Luke's. He squeezes them, enjoys her touch, then feels bad for taking pleasure while their soldier friend is marooned and in danger.

The UAV over their heads is stationary. If it advances another ten feet, it'll be able to see them, but as long as it remains in place, they're safe. However, while the spiteful machine is there, watching the courtyard and wasteland, Luke, Jada and Brad can't help Floyd. So they're at an impasse. Meanwhile, inside the flat, Lena is dying. Any hope of bringing the Government to justice will probably perish with her.

Is that my problem, though? Lena's not the only person in there who needs 'elp. Connor. My first responsibility should always be to 'im. I should be takin' 'im to the countryside, gettin' away from all this shit, these fuckin' zombies, these ugly tower blocks 'n' burnt-out cars. To Atherbury, checkin' Dad, Maddie 'n' Mason are okay while I'm at it.

He thinks of Lena's ghostly-white flesh, her sweat-drenched face. Hopefully, she's delirious and isn't suffering too much. *But she's partly t' blame fer all this. 'Er own injury. Floyd stuck out there. Floyd's mate dead. All this pain. 'N' we're riskin' life 'n' limb to 'elp 'er.*

Jada grips his hand tighter. He remembers he's not sustaining Miss Adderley merely for own sake. Exposing the truth behind the apocalypse is important to her and Brad, and therefore to Luke as well. *But is it worth riskin' Connor's life? Or should 'im 'n' me just leg it? Then what about Brad? 'N' Jada? There could be somethin' between us. 'N' I could be runnin' away from it. Imagine if I found out, later on down the line, that she died, that I might've saved 'er if I'd stuck around. Plus I'd be abandonin' m' mate. Brad's already lost 'is daughter. I can't leave 'im too.*

Effectively, if he survives the next hour or so, Luke has a choice. He can be a father, but *only* a father, putting Connor's safety above all else. Or he can be a member of the team, a cog in the machine.

Both options have advantages and drawbacks. For a start, if he and Connor were independent, they wouldn't be in this fix now. Locked in a block of flats with a dying woman and a schizophrenic, surrounded by zombies and flying terminator robots. If everyone else were gone, though, would the father and his son still be alive? Keeping under the radar is all well and good, but once the undead have their scent, their hours are numbered.

"Brad," Jada says, "can you see Floyd?"

Lying alongside the railings, Brad's at most risk of being spotted by the drones, but he also has the best view. "Still under that car, I think."

"He's okay, right?" While Luke might've been having disloyal thoughts of fleeing with his son, he still hates the idea of Floyd dying after seeing his comrades safely into the tower block. *I'm not a total piece o' shit.*

"Think so. But… shit… there's zombies 'eaded 'is way."

"The drones'll kill 'em, surely?" Jada says. She receives an almost immediate answer when the UAV over the wasteland opens fire.

Luke cranes his neck to get a better look: the meandering monsters are swiftly transformed into broken body parts on the dusty floor. The next group to risk their guts for a taste of survivor receive similar treatment. "Jesus. They just don't give a fuck, do they?"

"Not when they're 'ungry," Brad comments.

"I wonder if they're ever sated?" Jada wonders. "I mean, say they had unlimited food, would they just keep eatin' an' eatin' forever? Where would all the food go? Do they even *digest* it? Would they get fat?"

"Dunno." Luke sighs. "I keep thinkin' o' questions like that. Like —"

"Shit." Brad points. "One of 'em's still alive. Movin'. Lost a leg but crawlin'."

Again Luke chances adjusting his position to see for himself. "Why's the drone not firin'?"

"Outta ammo, maybe." With some difficulty, Brad gets his rifle into to use the scope without it protruding between the bars. "It's just watchin' 'im."

Jada gulps. "Now there's more zombs on the way."

Up above, motors buzz, and the second hunter/killer crosses the courtyard at some speed.

Shit. Floyd needs t' defend 'imself. But killin' the zombs'll give away 'is position t' the new drone. Shit.

Chapter 59 — Jada Blakowska — 08:20

She's up on her feet, heedless of Luke's pleas for caution. Jada doesn't have any ideas. She's no more likely to come up with any by standing up, but she can't lie down while Floyd gets slaughtered.

A face appears at the French windows, making her jump. "Theo? Stay inside."

He ignores her and opens the sliding doors. "What's goin' on?"

"Just get back inside, Theo."

"No! I want t' know what's 'appenin'. Is Floyd okay?"

With a sigh, Jada explains the situation.

Gabriela's been listening too. "There's gotta be somethin' we can do."

"Shoot the zombs goin' fer 'im." Theo's at the balcony railings. When Luke and Brad don't respond, he adds: "Gimme a gun, 'n' I'll do it."

"Don't be daft." Stung into action, Luke aims and fires, as does Brad. The range is long; they expend a full clip between them before the enemy is beaten.

"What about that drone?" Gabriela asks.

"Which one?" Jada frowns. "There's two."

"No," Theo says, "she means the one we found inside. It's one o' them remote control ones."

"So? What use is that to us?"

"I… dunno." Theo shrugs. "Maybe —"

"— We can use it to distract the drones!" Gabriela does a little hop.

Theo's already heading back inside. He re-emerges thirty seconds later with a miniature unarmed version of the hunter/killers in one hand and a tablet device in the other. He swipes the screen of the latter to reveal a close-up image of Brad's face. "Got its own tab. See." When he sets down the mini-drone on the balcony's table, Luke appears on the display instead. "I've got a plan." He taps at the tablet and grins as the gadget hums into life.

The adults look impatient, but Gabriela claps her hands. Connor and Evie are at the window now, intrigued.

Approximately the size of a shoebox, the UAV is deceptively quick. It's halfway to the wasteland when Jada asks what Theo's planning.

"What d'ya reckon the big drones'll do when they see mine?" the adolescent says.

"Shoot it?" she replies.

"Not the first one," Brad reminds them. "Outta ammo."

"But yeah," Luke adds, "the second one'll deffo shoot it down. Any second now…"

"It'll try." Theo's intent on the tablet screen now.

The second drone turns. Perhaps it's heard Theo's aircraft approaching, or maybe the first drone has made visual contact and passed on the message.

Theo swipes the touchscreen, ordering the vehicle to bank hard right, just as the enemy machine opens fire. Above the survivors, windows shatter, and concrete splinters as misaimed cannon rounds pepper the building. The smell of dust is strong.

Gabriela squeals with delight.

"Jeez, Theo," says Luke. "'Ow ya know it was gonna fire then?"

Brad nods his approval. "Mad skills, bro."

Beaming, Theo pilots the mini-drone past its still-firing, relatively-cumbersome counterpart. "Now watch." His toy swerves left, heading for the UAV closest to Floyd.

Turning, the other continues to spit shells. Its stream of fire gets closer as Theo's machine loses velocity.

"Runnin' outta charge?" Jada asks, arms folded. "'Cause if it is, what exactly have ya gained?"

Suddenly, Luke pushes himself off the railings towards Theo. "What are you doin'? Yer gonna —"

The rumbling cannonade is abruptly masked by the crackle of riddled steel as the firing drone, still tracking Theo's, shoots its ammunition-less colleague by accident. A muted explosion follows.

Shit.

"Everyone inside!" Brad says.

"What?" Theo was expecting praise, so he's confused. "I still need t' lead the second drone away, 'n' give Floyd chance to escape."

"You'll have to do it inside." Jada practically drags the two teenagers off the balcony. Once inside, she pulls the curtains closed and dims the lights. At least there's not much furniture in the flat to trip over. Judging by the single pouf and gaming system, plus the aroma of dirty dishes, its tenant was a single adult.

Ashara and Gould, sat at a shabby breakfast bar, don't react to the sudden darkness – she looks exhausted; he's muttering to himself – but Connor and Evie are up on their feet, wanting to know what happened outside. So Luke explains. Brad, using his rifle scope, peeks through a gap in the curtains. Meanwhile, with Gabriela watching, Theo's still fiddling with the tablet.

Jada eyeballs the latter. "D'ya not remember, last night, us tellin' ya what happened when we disabled that drone at the chemical factory?"

The youth blinks, looks at Gabriela for support. "Uhh… when you broke its gun, right, then ran away?"

Gabriela bites her lip. "Oh dear."

"Everyone get down on the ground," Jada orders; they obey. "Ashara! Not under the light."

Theo, the stereotypically impulsive yet dopey teenager, finally realises the potential ramifications of his stunt and stands up. "Oh, no… they bombed ya, didn't they?"

"Mm-hm." Already on her knees, Jada grabs the boy's sleeve and yanks. "Now get the fuck down!"

"What about Floyd, though?"

"He was probably listenin' last night." *Unlike you.* "An' he'll be makin' sure he's safe."

"Is he?" Ashara's voice trembled. "Is he movin'?"

"Uhh… not that I can see…" Brad rubs his eyes and looks again.

"Idiot!" Gould proclaims, though it's unclear whether he's referring to the soldier out in the open, or the lad who may have unwittingly summoned an air strike.

Everyone is quiet for a few heartbeats. As Brad shifts position, a beam of sunshine illuminates tired, drawn faces. Dust motes dance in the light.

"Has he moved yet?" Luke asks.

"No."

"Brad, come away from that window," Jada says. "There's nothin' ya can do to help him, anyway. If, *when* the air strike lands, you'll be shredded to ribbons standing there."

"Just gimme one more second…"

"'Ow long was it, last time?" Luke has an arm around both Connor and Evie. "Before the missile 'it, I mean? Musta been, what, two minutes —"

"— He's on the move!" Brad exclaims. "Leavin' the wasteland behind —"

"— Awesome!" Luke gestures. "Now get outta the window, fer fucksake!"

His friend moves. And that's when the boom comes.

The women and children yelp in fear. Grunting, Brad throws himself across the room. Cringing, Jada covers her ears. Then she realises: they're safe. The explosion wasn't as loud as anticipated, and the window is intact. She gets up, pulls apart the curtains, opens the sliding doors and searches for Floyd. The others gather around and behind her.

The Army targetted the wrong building. Smoke pours from the other side of Chamberlain Heights.

Yes! Fuckin' yes! Jada almost smiles, until she remembers Floyd. *He didn't run there, did he? It's not far from the wasteland…*

The single gunshot has them all looking back towards the woods. In the distance, an ant-sized Floyd is gunning down a second zomb. Now he's sprinting to the trees.

"There's too many of 'em there!" Brad complains. "Shitloads still comin' from the canal…"

"Yeah, but…" Jada hopes Floyd's had the same idea as her. Because the surviving enemy drone is on the move once more.

"What?" asks Luke, using another rifle to watch the soldier, who's shooting a pair of undead. Another three swerves his way; he ignores and passes them, as though he wants to be surrounded. The trio are in hot pursuit, but Floyd makes it to the tree he used as a sniper's nest.

Four separate groups are converging on Private Nelson's position. As is the UAV.

Jada wipes perspiration from her brow. "I think he's gonna —"

"— Use the zombies to distract the drone?" Gabriela wonders.

"Then I'll give 'im a hand!" says Theo, who, like the enemy drone, has forgotten the gadget he was piloting. He flies his toy at its weaponised counterpart. The latter alternates between trying to shoot down the former and blasting canal-soaked freaks.

Spotting his opportunity, Floyd jumps down from the oak. The Army drone realises its mistake too late. A couple of minutes later, its quarry is beneath the balcony. He's dragged to safety just in time.

For an ear-splitting moment, the hunter/killer, now ignoring Theo's pesky distraction, riddles the apartment block with cannon-fire. Glass shatters. Concrete cracks. Plasterboard is torn to shreds. Flat on her belly by the gaming chair, Jada covers her ears. Grits her teeth against the dust. Prays for an end to the cannonade. Hopes no one's been hit.

When the gun falls silent, the silence is almost palpable. The others are coughing, spluttering. But, miraculously no one's crying in pain, for it was the flat *above* that was targetted. Lips trembling, she rises to her knees. Everyone is unscathed. Physically, at least. Shell-shock has rendered them mute.

Until Theo speaks: "It's goin'. The drone." He's watching the mini-UAV's feed on the iPad.

"Must be outta ammo," Floyd concludes.

"You good, bro?" Brad asks.

"Yeah. I'm good."

"We owe you one. Big time," says Luke.

"No biggie, fam."

What now?

The survivors talk. They need to do something to help Lena: find a pharmacy, or a hospital, and get some medicine before the sepsis kills her and destroys any proof of government culpability for the outbreak. Also, however, they have the kids to worry about; scouring the streets in such a large group would be suicide.

"Listen, Jada." Luke, sitting next to her, holds her gaze for a moment. "I know Lena's important t' you. T' you as well, Brad," he adds when his friend looks about to interject. "But I need t' keep Connor safe. We need t' keep *all* the kids safe."

"Is it safe 'ere, dough?" Floyd is checking the guns, making sure they're all loaded. "Dat last drone knows we here, innit."

"Hopefully, they think they killed us." It's the first time Gould's spoken for a while. His eyes are bloodshot, his cheeks drawn. "Though it's weird that they fired too high. Like they just wanted to scare us. Anyway, I'm staying put. I'm not being chased around the streets by any more of those zombie fuckers, if I can help it."

"I'm stayin' too." Ashara's voice is shaky. "I'd only slow ya down."

Luke has one arm around his subdued son's shoulders. His other hand clasps Jada's, squeezing almost tight enough to hurt. Neither man nor woman blinks; they don't want to be parted. Although they have other priorities, separating would be a wrench.

Christ, we've only known each other forty-eight hours. Feels like months.

"Perhaps ya could jus' stick around fer a bit," he says airily. "Ya know, make sure there's not loadsa soldiers bein' sent 'ere. Ya could be walkin' straight into a trap."

Brad raises his eyebrows in exasperation. *No point askin' him what to do. It's clear in his face. He wants to get out there, do something, hit back at the people who caused his daughter's death. But we need to keep an eye on him. That kinda anger can lead to fuck ups.*

"I'll check on Lena," Ashara says.

The children are talking among themselves; Gould is talking to himself. While Luke is quiet, his eyes are saying everything.

I know, Luke. I feel it too. Brad's right, though. We need to do somethin'.

But Jada's scared as well. Last night, they were relatively safe, with four walls around them, and a roof over their heads. After a brief interlude outside, they're indoors again. The forces of darkness are kept at bay by bricks and mortar. Aside from being divided from Luke and the children, to whom she grows closer with every passing hour, she has her own mortality to consider.

All of a sudden, the decision is made for her. Lena's breathing has quickened, which, according to Ashara, could indicate septic shock, meaning death within hours.

So Floyd, Brad and Jada will strike out in search of medical supplies. The rest will stay in the flats.

Using Theo's mini-drone, they scout the surrounding area. The canal horde has dispersed somewhat, its members wandering aimlessly between the apartment buildings. With Floyd taking command, the outbound crew should be able to evade the pockets of monsters.

"I wish you weren't goin'." Squinting against the rising sun, Luke looks lost. Like an overgrown version of his son.

With one leg already over the balcony railing, Jada hesitates. "Me too. I wish I didn't *have* to go."

"You don't. Brad 'n' Floyd know what they're doin'. You don't need —"

"— I do. This is my... *thing.* It's my fight. I can't let them do it for me."

"Come on, Jada," Brad hisses from below.

"Okay." Briefly, Luke looks about to say something else: one final plea, perhaps. Then he sighs and stoops to kiss her cheek.

She almost intercepts and kisses his lips, but she blushes instead, then kisses his cheek.

"Take care," he says.

"You too."

Chapter 60 — Naomi Adderley — 09:45

Every sense is sharpened. Yet the one she needs the most, her hearing, is hampered by her own pounding pulse. She's never been so scared, not even when a bear charged her in Yellowstone Park last year. Of course, while none of her foes today are as formidable as the furry predator she shot in the head, there are *a lot* of them.

Maybe fifty outside on the motorway. A dozen in here, in the service station into which she fled a couple of hours ago. Naomi thought she was clever, getting out of the open and indoors. She wasn't as prudent as she thought, however. Because she's made a trap for herself. Twice she's been flushed out of hiding places – from behind the newsagent counter, and out of the burger bar kitchen – but next time will be the last, for she's backed herself into a corner.

It's pitch black in the janitor's store cupboard, with the faintest sliver of light visible in the door's crack. Naomi's left foot is damp; she kicked over a half empty mop bucket when she bundled into the hidey-hole thirty minutes ago. Shifting position, she winces at the squelch of her sodden shoe. *Do they have superhuman hearing? Those disgusting monsters out there, are they super-powered? Are they* supernatural, *or just mindless freaks?*

Squeezing her eyes closed, she tries to recall Panucci's warnings. Her brain's not functioning correctly, though; its inner workings are petrified by fear.

Come on, Adderley. Get it together. That grizzly weighed over 650lbs, and it was running at 35mp/h, the tracker guy said. Nearly a third of a tonne, bearing down on you, all fangs and claws and muscle, but you aimed and fired like it was nothing. So why are you shitting your knickers now?

Maybe because today she's not armed with a Mossberg 500 pump-action shotgun. Nor does she have Jefferson Wagner at her shoulder, with his own 12-gauge, ready to lend a hand.

You're on your own, kid. No Jefferson. No daddy to call upon. All these years, she's mentally condescended to her sister Lena, scorning her for choosing the easy option by taking over the family business. Thinking she was somehow superior by striking out on her own. Except she never was truly alone, for she spent her father's money and used his connections.

None of that can help her now. Little Miss Adderley is in a building the size of a supermarket, with a multitude of animated corpses for company. Soon enough, they'll find her, and she'll be killed. Eaten. Only partially devoured, though, because at some point she'll rise from the dead herself. Then she'll be one of *them*, part of the undead army Panucci mentioned.

Footsteps on the corridor outside. Suddenly, Naomi's heartbeat is deafening once more, maddeningly loud, as though her own body is trying to sabotage her. *Calm down, Naomi. Just breathe. In and out, in and out. The zombie is walking away from you, not towards.*

Next time, she might not be so lucky. She needs to make a move, take action, do something. She's an Adderley, and cash isn't the only thing she's inherited. Her mother always said she was the tougher of the two daughters, that she had more of her dad's steel running through her veins. So she needs to stop being a coward, escape Hathaway Services and its ungodly denizens, find a way to Manchester, save her sister, get to somewhere safe.

The next sixty seconds she spends making a conscious effort to slow her breathing. Her heart rate slows as a result; she can now focus on her senses and think logically. When facing an adversary, one must use one's own strengths and exploit the other party's weaknesses. *What are their weaknesses? Apart from stinking like roadkill and looking like Halloween revellers?*

They're noisy. The opposite of stealthy, they presumably catch their prey by instilling panic, by overwhelming with numbers, by forcing people into corners, but a smart operator like Naomi should be able to run rings around these oafs. She won't do so by cowering away in here, though.

She licks her lips, tastes the salt of sweat and tears. *Breathe in. Breathe out. Stay calm.* She listens and hears nothing nearby, though the sound of rampaging zombies elsewhere in the complex is unmistakable. Taking one final breath, Naomi turns the closet door handle. Her stomach convulses as the hinges creak for a millisecond.

The service station's lighting is stark and unforgiving. Eyes narrowed, she looks left – bloodstained gents' bathroom door, bloodstained ladies' bathroom door, crimson streak on the grey linoleum floor – and then right – a skill crane game, its lights flashing and soft toys grinning despite the horror, and a drinks vending machine. Then a left turn signposted 'EXIT/DINING AREA'.

Breathe in. Breathe out. Stay calm.

She steps into the corridor. Glass smashes in the men's room; she gasps. *Breathe in. Breathe out. Stay calm.* Every instinct screams "run!" But she needs to take her time. So she creeps to the right. One foot after the other, every footfall more leaden than the last as she passes the vending machine. When she reaches the 'exit' sign she stops.

Again she wills herself to be brave. A peek around the corner inspires both hope and despair: the main entrance doors aren't as far away as she remembered, yet the lobby isn't empty. Three ghouls are present. Wet munching sounds and a foul reek set the scene.

The closest, an obese, Liverpool FC jersey-sporting white male in his forties, stands before the newsagent's. Rocking from one foot to the other, it stares at the ceiling as if conversing with God. Number two is by the revolving doors at the exit. Once a twenty-something Asian woman, the fast food chain uniformed beast is missing an arm. Or rather, it holds its detached arm with the other hand, dribbling blood onto the floor. The third enemy, a blonde ponytailed infant, is on all fours, its face buried in the guts of an already-ravaged old man. The white of ribs coated scarlet by gore has Naomi covering her mouth.

Don't throw up. This is no place for a weak stomach. Breathe in. Breathe out. Stay calm.

She takes a risk by leaning further into the open. Outside, there are stalled vehicles and humanoid figures. If she can get past the three zombies, perhaps she can steal one of the cars or vans. There's a 4x4; she can drive it through the fields to the rear of the rest stop instead of negotiating the traffic jam on the M6.

Asian freak looks her way. Naomi's chest freezes. Her throat constricts. The bleeding, drooling creature lets out a sound like a deflating tyre and takes one heavy step in the human's direction, and then another.

Eyes flitting from one monster to the next, the woman screams inside. Thus far, only the fast food zomb has registered her presence. But after five hesitant steps from their alert comrade, the other two take a look for themselves. The red-chinned, feasting child stares, unblinking. Fat football fan lurches forward.

Oh, fuck.

Letting out the faintest of whimpers, Naomi backs away. She backs into the claw machine. Casting around for inspiration, she finds none. Until she spots a fire extinguisher on the wall opposite the arcade game.

By the time she's detached the device from its housing, the rotund zombie is almost upon her. Arms reaching, fingers flexing, its tongue protrudes between ragged, chewed-at lips. Naomi grunts as she swings her rudimentary bludgeon. The impact sounds like knuckles on a frying pan. A tinkle: teeth hitting the ground.

The beast falls like a tree, landing heavily on its would-be breakfast.

Naomi yelps, reels away, almost loses her footing. Instinct takes over as she hurdles the downed assailant and sprints for the exit. Asian zomb drops its dismembered arm and stumbles to intercept. It's too slow. Undead child springs to its feet, but Miss Adderley pays it no heed.

She piles through the turnstile. Blinks in the sun. In her peripheral vision, there are zombies taking note, necks twitching, backs stiffening, like dogs sniffing hares. Steps are heading her way, from behind, from right and left. Amidst the parked vehicles, figures move. The dead are coming to life.

Bike. Against a rest, but not chained to it. Keys in the ignition? Yep.

She's only travelled by motorcycle twice, and on one of those occasions she rode pillion. *Fuck it.* Mounting, starting the engine and driving away come as easily as riding a bicycle. Within a few heartbeats, she's speeding away on the black Honda, the wind cool on her brow, frustrated dead walkers in her wake.

Weaving between halted cars, Naomi soon escapes the snarl-up. She heads south-east for Manchester, her mind as empty as the motorway. After approximately five kilometres, she pulls over and vomits. For a moment, she does nothing but dribble bile onto the tarmac.

Jesus Christ. Panucci was right. This is fucking crazy.

Suddenly she feels giddy. Unlike the poor souls left behind at the service station, she's still alive. She's free. Naomi still has a job to do, however, a sister and family to save. Spitting one last time, she restarts the motorbike and rides on. Before long, she spots aircraft in the sky; they're not all chemical-spewing aeroplanes, though. *Machine-gun drones, like Panucci said.*

She's making good time till she reaches the Greater Manchester borough of Wigton. Again, the M6 is blocked by traffic, except that on this occasion, the cars are all empty. There's no sign of the undead, though a couple of vehicles have smashed windows and dented doors. Half a mile back, she passed an exit, so she turns the bike one hundred and eighty degrees and goes back the way she came.

Holborne is one of those strange semi-rural yet industrialised spots common in this part of the world. Certain streets might've been pleasant ten years ago, but skeletalised trees give it a melancholic air. At least the air is a little fresher. The streets are quiet, and Naomi is almost clear of the centre before she sees people.

The elderly couple regard her with suspicion when she slows to a stop by the pavement. Their dog, an adorable Pomeranian, seems more trusting.

"Hey." Naomi clears her throat. "Excuse me, but do you know the best way back to the motorway? I'm trying to get to Mortborough."

The old man scratches a bald, sunburnt head. "Back that way, love."

"No, sorry, I mean without using that junction. It's blocked. Tons of cars, just stopped in the middle of the road. You wouldn't know anything about that, would you?"

After scolding her curious pet, the woman studies Naomi. "Terrorists, they keep sayin' on't news."

"Aye, but we've seen nowt," the man adds. "Brexit was s'posed t' stop these terrorist buggers, but it's worse than ever now."

"Everybody's stayin' indoors." The woman lowers her voice. "Everybody's scared t' death."

Naomi shifts position on the bike. "So you haven't seen anyone… acting strangely?"

"Tha's askin' the wrong people, love." The lady turns away and tugs on the Pomeranian's leash. "We mind our own business."

The elderly gentleman shrugs an apology. "If tha' keeps on through Hinceley, tha'll see signs fer Mortborough. Some o't roads are shut, mind."

"Thanks." Naomi turns the ignition key, then starts at the sound of gunfire in the distance. Watching the pensioners hurry down a driveway, she has a thought. She needs to speak to Panucci to arrange collection of the weaponry he's sourcing for her. When she dials he doesn't answer; she feels icicles of fear in her bosom. *Hopefully, he'll ring back. If he's still alive.* She revs the bike's engine and continues east.

Two minutes later, she see signs for Hinceley. After a set of dysfunctional traffic lights and a left at a roundabout, she joins a broad A-road. And that's where she screeches to a halt. The collection of figures, forty metres away, look like soldiers. They're armed and wear fatigues. But would British Army be wearing black? Would they be pointing guns in the general direction of a random woman on a bike? Would they be standing around a corpse?

They look dodgy. They don't want me here, for some reason. Biting her bottom lip, she turns the Honda's handlebars, almost surreptitiously. Half a dozen rifles go from hip height to shoulder; someone shouts, "Don't move!"

Chapter 61 — Floyd Nelson — 10:35

"Listen, fam." Nostrils flaring, he pulls Brad back behind the fire-blackened telecoms van. "Don't wanna pull rank or nuttin', but just chill da fuck out, ya get me?"

"He's right, Brad." Jada's watching the road behind them, maintaining composure. "Floyd's the expert. If he says it's not safe, it's not safe."

The shorter man huffs. "I thought it was the ones in black we 'ave t' worry about. These look like regular soldiers t' me, bro. Just like you."

"Don't matter. Everyone's a enemy till we know better."

Automatic fire in three round bursts, just around the next corner. Lots of it, then running boots. *Dey gettin' dey arses whipped.* Floyd risks a peep through the van's driver-side window. The camouflaged men look panicked as they dash across a narrow sidestreet and into a back alley, with a score of bloodthirsty fiends close behind. One of the men, barely out of his teens, is limping, moving too slowly.

The watching deserter ducks down just as a scream signals the inevitable. "See," he says. "If we'd have followed you, Brad, we'd be dead now."

Salton's full of troops, most of them in His Majesty's uniform, but it's also home to hundreds of undead. The latter seem to be gaining the upper hand, with three of the four engagements they've witnessed thus far being won by Team Zombie. The mayhem means Private Nelson, Brad Li and Jada Blakowska have made little progress thus far.

When the sidestreet is confirmed to be clear – save for the ragged body of the unfortunate hamstrung then eviscerated kid – the three survivors proceed down Wargrave Road. The terraced houses to each side are scorched by flame. Their windows smashed are smashed, doors ajar. Dark red stains and trails on the pavement are a frequent sight, as are discarded toys, luggage and articles of clothing.

They're nearing a T-junction when an explosion sounds no more than two hundred metres away.

"Fuckin' warzone, bro." Brad pauses, not for the first time. He's been vacillating between rashly desperate to advance and wary of the slightest sound since they left the flats. *Shock's fuckin wid his head, innit.*

"We just need to stay alert," Jada says calmly. "Which way now, Brad?" Luke's friend knows Salton no better than her, by all accounts, but she's clearly trying to force him to focus on the mission.

"Ahh… where are we now?"

Floyd casts left and right and sees a charred street sign by a blackened pickup truck. "Westmoreland Road."

"Gould said the Quays, right?"

"Yeah." Jada clicks the walkie-talkie to confirm. "Gould, do you read me? Over."

The transport worker, back at the flat, is presumably still seated at the tenant's computer he hacked. He's been guiding them since Theo's drone ran out of charge, but he can't help them now. His reply is a garble of nonsense.

"Fuckin' stupid thing." Jada glares at the device. "What's wrong with it?"

"Problem wid da signal, not da radio." Floyd's still looking in the direction of the signpost; his gaze lingers on a dead soldier in the gutter. The dark-skinned man has a beard. *Like Gurd. Poor bastard died 'cause o' all dis shit.* Any fatigue he'd been feeling evaporates, burned away by anger. "Come on. Let's keep goin'. Road be clear for a bit."

The private leads the way, keeping low, remembering his training. A quick glance over his shoulder tells him his companions are aping his movements. Brad points right when they reach an intersection. The next street isn't as shaded as Westmoreland; the shattered remains of a wrecked bus stop twinkle in the sun. Floyd squints, licks sweat from an increasingly-stubbled top lip.

A crackle from his rear has his heart thundering, but it's only Jada's radio. They take cover behind a minibus that's crashed into a telephone exchange box.

"Gould?" she pants. "Gould, do you read me, over?"

"Reading you. What's your location? Over."

"Ahh…"

Brad points. "Lime Avenue."

"You get that?" Jada asks. "Over."

"Got it. Hang on a mo'." *Checkin' da map.* "Right. You're not far from Salton Quays. The pharmacist is pretty much bang in the middle. You know that grill place? Over."

"Yeah." Jada makes a face. "All the wings you can eat for twenty quid. Got food poisonin' there once."

"That's a very helpful anecdote, Jada. Anyway, the pharmacist is over the road from there. In front of a tram stop. Over."

Footsteps on asphalt. The crunch of glass underfoot. Within thirty yards.

"'Ow we get from 'ere t' there?" Brad asks.

"Follow Lime Avenue for fifty metres. Left onto Falkland —"

"— Second left —" Luke interrupts.

"— Sorry, *second* left. Then you'll be on Monarch Road. Takes you all the way into the Quays. Over."

There's a hacking, viscous sound, like a chain-smoker first thing in the morning.

"Thanks, Josh. And Luke. You okay?"

Her voice is tuned out. It becomes white noise in the background, secondary to that of footfalls and the rustle of clothes. Soon she falls silent.

Brad meets his eye. *He knows. No gunfire unless absolutely necessary. Don't need to attract no attention.*

The smaller man goes left, to the rear of the Ford Transit; Floyd goes the other way; Jada peers through the vehicle's spider-webbed rear cabin window.

Private Nelson takes the briefest of looks over the phone exchange: two zombies. The one on his side wears hi-vis clothing and a hardhat over a mess of unruly curls. Its partner was a woman once, an office worker judging by the sensible haircut and white blouse.

No big deal. He lowers his rifle and indicates that his comrades do likewise. Brad hefts his axe. Floyd nods. *I'll take da other one. Bounce it wid da butt o' my rifle. Jada... good girl.* She's got the message; she'll cover them with her gun.

Right. Smash it right in da mouth. Den Brad can finish it wid da axe. Once he's done his.

Wordlessly, he raises three fingers. Lowers one, then another, tenses inside, breath held —

His zombie's head explodes. A rifle cracks almost simultaneously, taking responsibility for the kill. Brad's mark freezes, a blossoming red flower between the breasts. Shot number two is swiftly followed by a third. The staggered female zombie's throat erupts. It too sinks to its knees, claret saturating a newspaper on the ground.

"Get down!" Floyd hisses. He drops to his belly, hears the others do the same, then manoeuvres himself into a position giving him a view past the exchange box. Every sense is on overdrive. His vision in crystal clear HD. The buzz of flies over a pool of blood. A rotten reek on the wind. Using his gun's scope, he searches the road ahead. He sees no movement between the terraced houses. Except, wait... no, just a dog. A living one. Blinking perspiration from his eyes, Floyd shifts his body; a crushed cola can was digging into his ribs.

There are plenty of hiding places in his line of sight. Empty saloons. Burnt-out hatchbacks. Overturned vans. Plus, the upper floors of the homes either side of the street would be excellent vantage points for a sharpshooter. *Dey won't be lyin' in wait, dough. Dey'll be on some sorta mission.*

A flicker of movement to the left. Aiming his rifle, Floyd spies a figure through a SUV window. Wearing black, the paramilitary is aiming a longer-barrelled weapon, a marksman's tool. *Won't be flying solo. So where's his boys?* He pays particular attention to the other parked vehicles near the 4x4. *There ya are, bitches.* Huddled behind a mangled convertible are two men in black. And, not too far behind, there are more, at least three of them, their machine guns resting on a pickup's flatbed. Private Nelson and his Mortborough friends are outnumbered two to one. Their enemies have more training and better leadership.

No thanks.

"Retreat!" Floyd hisses. "We'll find another way 'round."

As soon as he moves, however, the long range rifle fires again. Air hisses from a punctured minibus tyre. *Shit.* He looks around; the closest house is feet away. *In dere, out da back, over da wall.* He hand-signals his intentions, and the others act with alacrity. Another large calibre sniper round hits the Transit, then a second the telephone exchange box. They're inside by the time the third attempt cracks the doorframe.

"Quick!" Floyd leads the team through a gloomy home that hasn't been decorated since the 1960s. Blood splatters the kitchen's tiled floor, but there are no corpses. Heavy, plodding footsteps sound above them. Floorboards creak. The timber back door is locked. No key in sight. A single blow from Brad's axe grants egress, and they're outside again, under the intensifying sun.

His adrenaline's pumping, yet Floyd knows he needs to be cool. Fast, not hasty. The thunder of heavy boots from the road on the other side of the house is getting louder, however.

Brad's already kicking down the back gate. With a last look through the kitchen window, Nelson follows the other two into an alley. To their right, three undead are feasting on the carcass of a dog. To their left, fifteen yards away, a single zombie loiters. By the time it's stung into action, Floyd's already got it in his rifle sights. Its head explodes with a gratifying pop; the shot alerts the caninovorous trio.

"Run!" the AWOL serviceman yells.

They do. To the end of the ginnel, then right, into another street of terraced houses, another right. They pass pockets of dead men and women. Thrice guns are fired in their direction, the third striking a metal fence, at the end of a cul-de-sac, that the group are forced to scale.

"Canal." Brad pants, hands on hips. *He quick as fuck, but stamina not so hot.*

Floyd's studying the anorexic trees on the other side of the water: he sees no movement.

"Should lead to the Quays, right?" Jada's looking left and right. "If we go… left."

Five minutes of relative safety later, the walkway begins to rise, leaving the canal to run through a tunnel. There's a road either side of the bridge, a high wall straight ahead. Turning left takes them around a corner and along a highway bordered on its right by a grass verge that drops steeply.

The three survivors stop at the edge. Below them is Salton Quays, a sprawling commercial hub that was once an industrial powerhouse, a destination for ships from all corners of the globe. A quarter of a mile away, the dock waters glitter in the sun. Twentieth century docking cranes stand sentry, dwarfed now by the upmarket apartment towers, hotels and skyscrapers rented for exorbitant rates by multinational corporations and residential tenants with more cash than sense.

It's not the jungle of brilliant glass buildings and concrete constructions which grab their attention, however. Amidst the flats, offices, restaurants and banks there are hundreds of humanoids. Most are still, as though captured by one of LS Lowry's drawings. But some wander between haphazardly parked cars and trams.

Gunshots sound from the Quays every few seconds. Fires, smouldering here and there, add a smoky surrealness to the vista. The wind's blowing towards the watching trio, spicing their air with the stench of burning plastic.

"Looks like hell," says Brad, arms folded.

"I'm gettin' used to that." Jada starts down the slope.

Chapter 62 — Jada Blakowska — 11:15

"Well, that worked out well." Brad's deadpan. His expression remains neutral even when a zombie head thuds against the window inches from his head, leaving a red smear on the pane. Suddenly, a German Shepherd's foaming mouth appears; its saliva turns the bloodstain pink. This time, Brad does recoil.

Jada takes a moment before replying. "*I* didn't know there'd be shitloads of 'em in that in that office, did I?"

"No, course not." Brad shrugs. "Not sayin' it was a bad idea, am I? We need t' get those meds, 'n' this is the closest place, innit? 'N' when that office emptied, we 'ad no choice other than to 'ide in 'ere."

Floyd hasn't spoken since they dove into the empty tram a mere one hundred and fifty yards from the bottom of the grass verge. He's just finished checking the doors and windows. Now he's staring into the horde of undead surrounding the carriage, his eyes flickering left, right, up and down.

Well, it's not quite a 'horde', is it? There are at least thirty o' the ugly fuckers, more than enough to tear us to pieces if they get in, but it could be worse.

Indeed, their prospects would worsen considerably if more of the Quays' unholy denizens realised lunch had walked into their territory. If the number of hostiles doubled, or quadrupled even, there might be enough to break into the tram.

That's probably how this'll end. More o' them'll turn up. They'll push the tram over. Smash all the windows. Pull us out, one by one, screamin'...

She can't allow herself to abandon hope. Jada needs to stay positive, because despair will only cloud her thinking and prevent her from devising a way out of this mess.

But if Floyd, a certified bad-ass, can't come up with anythin', how can I? That's his job, kinda. Gettin' outta life-or-death situations. I'm only a reporter with a tendency to dig holes I can't get out of, an' Brad's just an IT worker with a grudge.

Looking at Floyd doesn't instil her with confidence. Normally unflappable, the squaddie seems panicked. Bereft of ideas. The day's growing warmer, but he's perspiring more than usual. Maybe he's reached the limit of his abilities. He's a rank-and-file soldier, trained to follow orders, to execute plans, not invent them. Being a crackshot with a rifle doesn't mean he's a strategic genius. He *wants* to act. His grip tightens on his weapon, trigger finger flexing, every time one of the dead monsters slams into the tram's exterior. Yet he doesn't know *how* to act. Private Nelson has become a wild animal: simultaneously afraid and angry; cornered and still desperate to lash out. A lion capable of mauling ten hyenas, but not a whole clan.

So what if no one comes up with a solution?

They will all die, of course. Then they'll either be resurrected to wander the streets, in hunt of prey as witless as they were while alive, or they'll stay dead and have their cadavers stripped to the bone. *Why do some people turn, an' others not? One day, scientists'll work it out, come up with a cure. But it'll be too late for us.* Either way, a painful doom awaits.

Plus, the Government will not be held to account. Knowledge of their culpability will die with Lena, unless a whistle-blower reveals the truth.

Maybe it was a lost cause all along. Jada watches a large, police uniform-wearing brute of a zombie lumber towards the tram. Its eyes blank, it almost seems like a machine, driven by an unconscious region of its brain. The closer it gets to the vehicle, the faster it moves. When its face slams into the window, the humans collectively wince, but the glass holds firm. Everyone breathes again.

Maybe we were always gonna fail. They were deluded to believe they could bring justice to the powers-that-be. Even if they healed Lena, the thousands of zombies, men-in-black and regular army would ensure they never escaped Greater Manchester. In the unlikely event they managed to prevail, they would likely be hunted and neutralised long before exposing Her Majesty's Government.

However, had Jada, Brad and Floyd stayed with the rest of the group and headed for the countryside, they might be safe by now. At Luke's father's house. Miles from the war zone and fires and explosions, free of the stench of putrefying flesh, with solid brick walls and sheer remoteness keeping their persecutors at bay. *Too late for that now. 'Cause soon, those gruesome bastards, with their grasping, mangled hands, and hungry mouths…*

"Didn't realise ya still 'ad a grenade left." Brad continues to stare out of the window, almost mesmerised by the pitter-patter of a redheaded boy-zomb's fingers on the glass.

"Was savin' it," Floyd replies, rehooking the frag to his belt.

"For us?" Jada asks, turning away from the big policeman zombie, who's standing ten yards from the tram, perhaps readying itself for a second charge.

"Yeah."

"Good." *Better to go like that, blown to pieces, than eaten alive.* "D'ya reckon it'll come to that?"

"If we can't fink of another way out, yeah. Not 'ow I expected to kick da bucket, but what can ya do?"

"I'm sorry."

Brad frowns. It's unclear whether he does so due to Jada's words or in response to the wiry, lycra-clad female fiend worrying at the frame of the carriage's sliding door. "What for?"

She shrugs. "Ya know. Bringin' ya both out here on this… fool's errand."

"It was my choice. I ain't got nothin' t' lose. 'N' I wasn't gonna run away wi' my tail between m' legs after what 'appened wi' LaRosa. No chance. I get the fuckers who caused this shit, or I die tryin'."

Floyd's nodding slowly. "No need to apologise. I knew da danger o' comin' out 'ere. 'N' I had my own score to settle, ya get me?"

"Gurdeep," Jada says softly.

The tall warrior says nothing, but his head drops.

Time passes at a snail's pace. At one point, the radio garbles into life, though the connection is too short-lived for Jada to apprise Gould of their dilemma. The briefest snatch of background noise is heard: a conversation between Evie and Connor. The little girl's voice hardens Jada's resolve. *That kid an' her brother have no one now. I need to make it through this, not just so Villeneuve gets what's comin' to him, but for Evie, and Theo, and Gabriela...*

Brad tries the walkie-talkie again, with no luck. "Damn thing's fucked."

Probably for the best. If Luke knows we're in trouble, an' he knows where we're in trouble, he'll probably come an' try to save us. Then he'll die too, an' leave Connor an orphan.

Because that's the kind of man Luke is. He may be reluctant to risk life and limb for Lena Adderley, but he would do anything to save his friends. Apparently, he's known Brad for five years, and despite only making Jada's acquaintance two days ago, there's a connection between two of them. *Isn't there? He does look at me a certain way, doesn't he?*

For a while, she forgets the fiends outside and daydreams. Although she laughs at herself internally, she imagines walking somewhere calm and peaceful with Luke. The sun high in the sky, a gentle breeze, birdsong, the ripple of a nearby stream, the aroma of freshly-mown meadows – real, living grass from five years ago, not pitiful yellow weeds. She and Luke grinning, chatting about trivialities. Connor seems like a good kid, and he's going to need a mother figure now. Evie, Theo, Gabriela too. They've all lost loved ones and will struggle with the aftermath more than anyone else.

Is that me, though, a replacement mum? Of course, Jada's thought about motherhood, but the concept has always been abstract, something intangible and distant, to be tackled when her career's been tamed. Maybe caring for the gaggle of youths she's collected will prepare her for real maternity. Luke seems like a good father…

You dick. None o' that is possible now. It's all gone to shit, all —

A boom nearby sweeps away the illusion's fractured pieces. The three refugees look towards the front of the tram: smoke is billowing from the single-storey office from which the tram-haunting zombies came. The explosion and resulting conflagration are attracting undead attention as well as that of the living.

Brad, suddenly animated, hurries to the front window. "Are they goin'?" He points. "Look, the zombs, that blast... it's distracted 'em."

"Hmm." Floyd hasn't moved; he purses his lips. "Not all o' dem. Not for long enough."

"You sure?" Jada's joined Brad. "Shit. You're right. They're losin' interest. Comin' back."

"Fuck!" Brad bashes the top of a seat with the heel of his hand. "We were too slow! Coulda got out, couldn't we? Too slow. Won't get another chance now." His expression mutates from ire to hopelessness. "Fucked it. We're gonna die in 'ere —"

"— That's enough!" Floyd snaps, eyeballing at the smaller man. "Get a grip o' yaself, bruv, ya get me?"

For a heartbeat Brad tenses, fists balled as if about to retaliate. Then his shoulders subside. He sinks into the frontmost passenger seat, moving slowly, like he's an old man.

"Sorry, Brad." Floyd squeezes his eyes closed. "Didn't mean to yell. Jus'... everyone's vexed. Everyone's..."

"I know. I know." Brad's voice is flat. "I'm sorry too."

"Okay. Let's jerk each other off later." Jada almost laughs. *Jeez, now* I'm *losin' it.*

The two men smirk, then chuckle. Soon, Jada's giggling as well. In a metal and glass box, surrounded by cannibals ravenous for their innards, in a city turned into a battleground by blackclad assassins, gun-drones and dead civilians.

"Just give me the fuckin' grenade," Brad says, still sniggering. "Let's die with a smile on our faces, at least."

Floyd shakes his head. "We ain't done yet, fam. No surrender. You in da army now. With me. Both o' ya. Consider me your recruitin' sergeant."

Brad salutes.

As does Jada, grinning even though she can see at least a dozen bloodthirsty enemies through the tram's window. Some of the zombies bang on the glass; others simply stare at their would-be prey. *Probably wonderin' what the fuck we're doin'. Is this how it ends for us? Goofin' 'round, smiles on our faces, then… bam! Painful death.*

Except they have the grenade, so they won't be anybody's lunch.

Hang on a min. The grenade. The explosion earlier. The distraction.

"Guys," Jada begins, "I think I've got an idea."

Chapter 63 — Randall Maguire — 12:05

Four hours. *Four fucking hours.*

Two hundred and forty minutes.

By now, Private Floyd Nelson could be anywhere. He could've escaped and caught a ferry to France in the time Maguire has been barricaded in this farmhouse. It would be funny were it not the lives of his family on the line: he and Jones are hiding from farmyard animals.

They escaped the herd of undead cattle easily enough, and when they saw the secluded stone cottage at the field's edge, their goal was simple. Take cover. Let the animals wander off somewhere. Re-emerge and continue the mission. However, as soon as they barred the ancient timber door, a crunching sound outside, along with a chorus of squealing, put their hopes to the sword. Pigs escaped their sty. Horses smashed their way out of a stable. Not long later, half a handful of human zombies arrived. Now Maguire and his bodyguard are marooned, trapped by an assortment of livestock and agricultural workers.

Bloody Jones is sat at the oaken kitchen table. The crisis hasn't affected his appetite; he's munching on bread, butter and a pungent cheese he declared to be 'heavenly'. "It's like a shitty horror film, isn' it, sir?"

"What?" Maguire, leaning on a mantelpiece above an authentic fireplace, blinks repeatedly, scouring away mental images of his family bound and hooded. "Horror film?"

"Yeah. 'Cept they wouldn't capture the *smell* in a film, would they? Used to wanna live on a farm, I did. But I always forget 'ow bad it smells."

"Hmm. D'ya know how long we've been stuck in here?"

"Yeah. Too long."

'Specially when it's your wife an' kids on the line. "We need to figure out an exit."

"Try air support again?"

"No. They said ninety minutes to reload an' recharge, an' that was an hour ago. The drones they did send've been shot down, presumably by the rogue forces at play. So we're gonna have to shoot our way out, I think."

Nodding slowly, Jones cuts himself another slice of dairy. "Looks like it. But, sir, with all due respect, ya came to that same conclusion, wi' the same reasonin', two hours ago."

"Yeah, well —" A thud from the front of the cottage silences the agent.

Pistol in hand, Bloody goes to check. He returns ten seconds later, eyebrows raised. "Door's still sound. Think it were that big horse, the brown an' white one. Beautiful creature. Or would be if it wasn't for 'alf its mouth bein' torn away."

"Did ya see any o' the human ones at the window?"

"No. I didn't wanna hang 'round, like."

"Anyway." Maguire pushes himself away from the chimney-breast. *I need to do somethin'. Can't cower away in here all day pretendin' discretion's the better part of valour.* "How many we facin'?"

"Dozen pigs? Give or take. Plus two horses, at least one dog, an' it looked like three humans. One of 'em's carryin' a pitchfork, like in —"

"— A film, yeah." *Jones seems like a capable soldier. Took out that chargin' bull without hesitation. But he's not a strategist, so I need to step up, an' do the thinkin'.* Maguire wants to pace, but he needs to stay away from the windows. "The good thing is, we're technically in Walkley, right?"

"Yeah."

"So Nelson, an' Adderley, they could be recoverable, if we can get outta this fuckin' buildin'."

Jones retakes his seat at the table. "I reckon so. I mean, between these zombie 'terrorists', zombie animals, an' rogue hostiles, the streets are pretty dangerous. Nelson, if he's got any sense, will be holed up somewhere. Jus' a matter o' time 'fore we find 'em."

They're both speaking common sense. The target has probably gone to ground, which means he's within reach. Rushing, losing their composure, will kill Maguire and his henchman as sure as any man-eating cow or man-in-black's RPG. And if he's dead, then his family will be snuffed out too. *Time is on my side. The bosses know this isn't an easy job, so I just need to chill out, take it slowly.* "How about this. We go upstairs. Get ourselves into a good snipin' position. Pick off as many o' the animals an' zombie humans as we can. Then we leave quick. Shoot our way clear."

"Not sure about you, sir, but I don't reckon I can outrun a horse, I don't. Or a Border Collie, for that matter."

"Okay. Good point." Maguire holds aloft the Toyota key Jones found earlier on the kitchen counter. "Whatever vehicle these are for, it's still here. In that garage across the yard, probably. Right?"

"Unless that's a spare."

"Yeah, well, we'll just have to hope it's the original, won't we?"

"That we will, that we will. So. Upstairs, snipe, out the door, shootin', to the garage, drive away. Yeah?"

Agent Maguire nods. With a plan in mind, he feels better already. He's been taught how to approach situations like this. The foes proposed in training weren't undead automatons, but their lack of intellect makes the zombies easier to conquer. *I'm smart. They're not. Brains always beats brawn.* "Right." He looks towards the staircase. "After —"

The jingle of breaking glass has both men reaching for their weapons.

Jones raises his left hand while holding his handgun with the other. "Stay behind me, sir. That was the front window, I'm guessin'."

Gulping back bile, Maguire follows his guard across creaking floorboards, into the house's hallway. He treads as lightly as he can. His ears strain. There's a scraping sound, like fingernails on wood. *Or glass on a windowsill.*

Now holding his Glock two-handed, assault rifle still strapped to his back, Bloody Jones pauses at the living room's threshold. The door is half closed. Most of the broad bay window is obscured. Tentatively, the lanky gunman pushes open the door with his boot.

Leaning right to see past his subordinate, Maguire holds his breath.

Thank fuck for that. Just one of 'em.

The dead farmer wears navy blue overalls stained black. Its pallid face is crusted dark red around the mouth and chin, its spectacles dotted with blood. With one arm poking through the shattered window, it reaches for a meal it hasn't yet seen. Then its frosty eyes flicker. Ragged lips peel away from slimy crimson teeth. The freak emits a gasping sound as it swings its left arm through the hole in the glass. Filthy fingers grip the inside windowsill.

The bang of Jones's pistol is deafening. A third crimson eye appears on the bridge of the zombie's nose; the back of its cranium vomits brain matter. Down slumps the invader, crunching glass beneath itself.

"Is that the only one?" asks Maguire dumbly. He can't see any others outside, though he can hear plodding steps.

"Don't know." Jones's chest heaves, but his arms are rigid. His handgun is steady, ready to slay the next attacker.

Claws scrabble. Hurdling the twice-killed human, a bundle of black and white fur and teeth enters the house. The Border Collie crosses the lounge before Jones can correct his aim. It leaps.

Caught between trying to fire and fending off the assault, the soldier does neither. Paws hit his shoulders and thighs. Jaws snap at his face.

Falling backwards, Jones manages to grip the canine by its throat. "Sir! Do something, sir!"

The words bounce off Maguire. He's in a bubble, a mere witness to the horrific scene before him rather than a participant. Detached, he stares at the person/dog hybrid on the beige rug.

"Help!"

Agent Maguire flinches as though slapped. He aims for the base of the sheepdog's skull. His gun booms; there's a wet popping sound. A hole appears in the carpet a couple of inches away from the downed man's shoulder. The animal collapses, supported now only by Jones's right arm.

Grunting, the prostrate bodyguard shoves the hound to one side and gets to his feet. "Shit. That was… fuck."

Maguire's staring at Jones's right sleeve, which is slickly scarlet. "Did it… *get* you?"

The taller man's eyes bulge as he follows his superior's gaze. "Oh, no, that's not my blood. I'm alright, I am. Thanks fer the save."

"No problem. Sorry it took so long."

"Ya froze. It 'appens."

A thump outside almost gives the pair whiplash. Both men point their weapons at the compromised window, but they see nothing. The clatter of horseshoes on paving stones is getting closer, however.

"Time to put that escape plan into action." Maguire switches his gun to his left hand and wipes sweat from his palm. For the first time, he registers the room's contents. A flat-screen TV lies face down on the floor; a coffee table is overturned, as are the three-seater and two-seater couches.

"'Ang on, sir." Jones wipes his sleeve on the living room's wall, staining the lime wallpaper red. "What if we get to the garage, an' there's no car in there?"

"Fuck knows. How about... new plan. Or, a tweak to the original. You leg it over to the garage. I'll watch out of a first floor window, distract any zombies who go after ya."

"Then ya cover my retreat if need be?"

"Exactly."

Glock ready, Maguire goes upstairs. His heart thunders in his skull. His vision throbs. Beneath him the front door clicks open as he enters the bedroom overlooking the yard. Across the room he creeps, stepping over bed sheets, articles of clothing and a dark stain. The sash window's fully open, so he props his elbows on the windowsill and trains his handgun on the gravel below. Opposite the farmhouse, the garage waits, with the stable ten yards to the right.

Coast is clear. Wait… is something there, to the left of the garage, behind that trough?

Movement in his peripheral vision. Directly below. It's only Jones, though, his gun swinging left then right.

Something moves again, by the trough. A red-mouthed pig, massive and hairy, trots into the open. Without hesitation, Jones blasts the beast; there's a thud as it hits the ground. Another one's coming, this time from the direction of the stable. Again the Welshman unloads, twice, bringing down another hundred kilos of rotten pork.

Should I be firin' too? Or just wait till he needs me?

Bloody Jones reaches the garage, which is padlocked. A single gunshot takes care of the lock, and he's swinging open the wooden doors.

Hooves on stone. An enormous horse is galloping, from the left, straight at Jones. He pushes the left-hand door wide, hoping to block the creature's charge, but it batters the obstacle to oblivion.

Fire, you idiot!

Maguire pulls the trigger five times: all but one of the rounds hits the target. The shire horse staggers, its white flank streaked crimson. Jones raises his gun, shoots the undead animal in the head and slips into the garage.

Blowing a long breath, Maguire waits. An engine starts, and his heart swells. *Yes! Fuckin' outta here.* He goes downstairs. Checks both ways when he reaches the door, sees a pair of scampering swine to the right, another one to the left snuffling at a corpse, Barry Jones to his front.

The Welshman stands next to an idling Toyota Landcruiser, pistol in hand. "Come on, sir! I've got ya covered."

Steeling himself, Maguire dashes to the garage. Twice his henchman looses bullets, once to each side. Both men dive into the 4x4, Jones in the driver seat. Tyres squeal; pebbles scatter. There's a crunch as a zombie hog runs into their path, and then they're clear. Joining the road, Bloody floors the accelerator. They leave the accursed farm behind and bear north.

"Fuck me." Maguire lowers the window, licks perspiration from his lips and squeezes trembling hands into fists. "Fuck. Me."

Jones is grinning. "That was intense, that was."

"Okay. Walkley now." The sun-drenched fields to either side of the highway give no clue as to their location, but the spire of a church is visible a mile away.

Maguire's pocket is buzzing – it's his personal mobile phone. Caylie's calling, which could be a good thing or a bad thing. "Hello?"

"Hey, hon. You alright?" His wife's mild Glaswegian tones soothe his soul.

"Aye. You an' Ronan okay?"

"Yeah, how's the conference goin'?"

"Fine. I'll be home ASAP. But listen, I'm a little busy right now, so I'll ring you later, right?"

"Sure. Just that… it's probably nothin', but…"

"What is it?"

She clears her throat. "There's a car outside —"

"— What kinda car?"

"Big, black, posh-lookin'. Why, what's the problem?"

Maguire bites his lip. "Nothin'. Just stay indoors, okay?"

"Why?" Caylie's voice raises an octave. "What's goin' on, Randall?"

"Nothin'... just, stay inside. You've been watchin' the news, yeah?"

"Yeah, but that's all in Manchester, right? Miles away."

"I know, I know. Probably just me bein' paranoid. But do me a favour anyway an' —"

"— Stay indoors. Okay, I get it."

They say goodbye.

Could be for the last time. The bastards're already set to make a move on Caylie an' Ronan.

Jones asks if everything's alright; Maguire lies again, mainly because he can't bear to voice his own fears.

He won't fail. He must not fail.

Chapter 64 — Luke Norman — 12:35

Hands on hips, he shifts from one foot to the other. "Gould. Ya said 'one minute' five minutes ago." *Jeez, I sound like I'm 'is dad.* "Come on. I'll be quick."

"Luke, I'm doing something important." The older man remains seated at the computer.

"What, exactly?"

"Footage of these men-in-black. Did I tell you I'm a skilled lip-reader?"

There's a surprise. "No. What's that got t' do with it?"

"I'm trying to work out what language they're speaking. You said the officer at the pub sounded Russian, didn't you?"

"Yeah. But I'm not that good with accents. He just sounded like one o' the characters in a video game I used t' play. But he's the only one I 'eard talkin'. Coulda just been 'im that was foreign, not all of 'em."

"Well, I've got good reason to be believe we're both right. You're right about him being Russian, and I'm right about them all being foreign. You see, there's a conspiracy theory about our government and the Russians —"

"— Christ, Gould, don't ya think we've got enough conspiracy shit t' think about?" He looks over his shoulder, at the kids and Ashara. With the curtains closed, the lights dimmed, their faces look drawn. "Now, fer the hundredth fuckin' time, can I use the fuckin' computer?"

Gould pushes away from the computer with theatrical disdain. The wheels of his chair whine. "It's all connected, Luke." He gets up, runs his hands off through his hair, indicates the PC. "Go on. It's all yours. Don't close any of those browser tabs, though."

Muttering a thank-you, Luke takes a seat. He searches for 'sepsis symptoms'. While he trusts Ashara's prognosis, he wants a better idea of how close Lena – who's laid-up in the bedroom, shivering – is to death. The medical sites he visits make for grim reading. By the looks of it, Miss Adderley is mere hours from death, and with her will perish any hope of exposing Villeneuve and his stooges.

Is it really important, though? As long as we all survive, so fuckin' what if the government gets away with it? Why can't someone else, someone without a kid t' think about fer a start, do all the cloak-'n'-dagger shit?

He leaves the desktop; Gould gladly takes his place. Walking into the kitchen, Luke rolls his neck and winces at the resulting cracks. *Don't need any o' this conspiracy or revenge bollocks. Just need a rest.*

As does everyone else. Fortunately, he, Ashara, Gould and the kids are benefitting from a temporary pause in the action. However, Jada, Brad and Floyd might not get their chance. Although the latter seems like a decent fellow, his untimely death wouldn't devastate Luke. If Brad never returned, the loss would be painful. As for Jada, the thought of her coming to harm is disproportionately troubling. Even though she only came into Luke's life two days ago. *Wanker. You're just thinkin' wi' yer dick.*

He pours himself a glass of water, forces it down his gullet and nibbles on a breakfast bar. Perhaps he should try the radio again. No, he decides; it's only ten minutes since he last attempted to communicate with his friends. They'll be in contact when they're ready. *If they're still breathin'...* Leaning on the kitchen sink, he strives to calm himself.

The hand on his back has him flinching and twisting.

"Sorry!" Ashara grimaces. "Didn't mean t' scare ya."

"'S alright. What's up?"

She sighs. "Just the kids. Connor 'n' Evie, they're a bit spaced out, like."

"Probably just in shock. Not surprisin', really." I *should be spendin' time wi' Connor, not indulgin' m'self 'n' leavin' 'im with a babysitter he's known fer a few hours*. Luke massages the bridge of his nose. "I'll 'ave a word wi' Connor. Evie was gettin' close t' Jada. 'Opefully she'll come back."

"She will. They all will." Ashara shuts the kitchen door and lowers her voice. "'N' Theo 'n' Gab, they're gettin… restless."

"What d'ya mean?"

The door opens. "If yer gonna talk about us, at least don't make it so obvious." The aforementioned teenagers are standing in almost identical poses.

"We're not talkin' about ya, Theo." Luke kicks his lips. "Well, we are, but not in a talkin'-behind-yer-back kinda way. More 'cause we're worried." *Fucksake. Never realised the apocalypse would involve dealin' wi' stroppy teenagers.*

Theo's chin juts out. "There's nothin' t' be worried about. We're old enough t' go out there 'n' do somethin' to 'elp."

"Do *what* to 'elp, exactly?"

"My uncle and cousins live in Liverpool," says Gabriela. "We want to warn them about this, to make sure they take it seriously."

"Can't ya do it on the computer? Message 'im on there?"

"He doesn't really use the Internet. He's paranoid about bein' spied on."

"He'll see it on the news, surely."

Now Gould is the kitchen door. "He won't. There's a complete media blackout. Plenty of rumours on social, but the news channels are claiming this is an 'ongoing terrorist' attack, pretending there's nothing for the rest of the country to worry about."

Shit. Does Dad know? He travels into Manchester once a week, usually Thursday, t' see old mates. Surely he'll know somethin' *is wrong…*

"Even on social media, any videos or posts telling the truth are quickly taken down," Gould continues. "The Government are still in full cover-up mode."

"See?" says Theo. "We need t' warn people."

Ashara shakes her head. "This could kill millions!"

"It certainly could." Gould's eyes bulge. "We need to do something about it. And I'm not talking about going to Liverpool to rescue a couple of people."

"What *are* ya talkin' 'bout, then?" Luke needs some space. The tiny kitchenette is too cramped. He walks into the lounge and over to the window, ruffling Connor's hair on the way without meeting the child's eye. The curtains remain all but drawn, but he can feel cooler air through a gap. Footsteps cross the floor behind him.

"We need to go to London." Gould's deep voice is calm, measured.

"*London*? Why the fuck would we go t' London?"

"I have a friend who works for the BBC. She can help us get the story out *without* Lena. Break through the wall of silence —"

"— Fucksake, Josh, we're strugglin' t' survive, 'ere. 'N' ya want us t' travel two 'undred miles —"

"— Out of the danger zone. Two hundred miles away from the walking fucking dead. We'd be safer —"

"— From the zombies, yeah! Not from the other bastards tryin'…" Luke looks at Connor and Evie, then at Theo, Gabriela and Ashara. He sees fear and uncertainty. "We could be followed. Those MIBs 'n' drones are everywhere. You *know* that, Josh."

"Still got to be better than this hellhole. With all those freaks out there." The older man points at the window. "How can you not see that?" His eyes narrow. "You know what, I don't think you're worried about being followed. I think you want your little girlfriend to be the one who gets the glory."

"What?"

"You want Jada to break this story, don't you?"

"Don't be ridiculous! I don't give a fuck *who* breaks any story. I just wanna keep everyone safe. Shit, if it was up to *me*, Jada, 'n' Brad, 'n' Floyd wouldn't even be out there, riskin' their lives."

"Yer bein' paranoid, Josh," Ashara adds. "Everyone's jus' doin' their best."

Shoulders slumping, Gould loses some of his zeal. "But you must understand. Telling the truth is *important*. It could save countless lives, as well as making sure those responsible get their comeuppance."

"Yer right." Luke frowns. There's a rumbling, squealing sound outside, and it's getting louder. "It *is* important. But *we* are too. So we'll do what we can t' get the word out, which is what Jada 'n' the guys are doin' now. But we'll also try t' survive, 'n' we got a better chance o' doin' that by stayin' in 'ere."

"What's that sound?" asks Ashara. She joins Luke at the window and peers through the gap between the drapes. "Shit."

"What's up?" Gould takes a look for himself.

Crossing the wasteland between the flats and the woods is a tank. It stops, its turret and cannon rotating. There's a boom, an explosion to the left, closer to another tower. Both Luke and Ashara turn to see a horde of undead. Body parts are scattered across the ground, but the hundred or so surviving zombies continue their march. Again the tank fires; again dead limbs, torsos and heads are torn asunder.

"There's more, look!" Ashara points.

A second mass of dead walkers is emerging from behind the third apartment block.

Infantry support wearing British Army uniforms overtake the battle tank. Now directly below Luke, they yell, gesticulate and bring their weapons to bear. Ripples of rifle fire thin the zombified ranks.

"There's some beneath us!" Gabriela points.

Just a few feet away, a pocket of zombs is moving to engage the soldiers. The tank adjusts its aim.

"Get back!" Gould barks.

The shell hits their tower underneath their storey, but it causes the floorboards and walls to shake. Connor and Evie cover their ears.

Wiping dust from his eyes, Luke coughs. "Jesus. That was close."

"Maybe it's not as safe in 'ere as we thought," Theo reflects.

He's right. We could easily become collateral damage sittin' in 'ere. The others look at him; he shrugs. "What can we do? Just need t' wait it out, 'n' 'ope fer the best."

Gould shakes his head and huffs. He seems about to argue when the radio buzzes on the computer table.

Luke trips over a coffee table, such is his haste to reach the device.

"Do you read me, over?" Jada's voice is a balm for Luke's fraught mind.

"We read you. Are you all okay, over?"

"Yeah. Just about. You guys? Over."

"Yeah, ta. Any luck findin' the pharmacist? Over."

"Yeah. But it's no good."

Luke rubs the back of his neck. "Why?"

"Place is -" Jada's voice is lost in static. "Over."

"What? I didn't get that. Over."

"- burnt out. Completely -"

"The pharm- gone. No -" The line goes dead.

"Hello? Jada, ya read me?" Luke suppresses an urge to hurl the walkie-talkie at the wall. "Shit!"

About two minutes after retaking his place at the PC, Gould sighs and nods at the screen, which displays a CCTV feed of a smoking building. "It's gone. The chemist at Salton Quays, just like she said."

Hands on hips, Luke stares at the monitor. "They need t' come back 'ere. Next time we speak to 'em, that's what we say."

"What about Lena?"

"Tough shit. They're gonna die out there, tryin' t' save 'er. Riskin' three lives t' save one, it's daft."

Another shell detonates outside as Luke's on his way to the kitchen to pour himself another water. The walls shake again; Evie screams, as does Connor.

"It's okay!" Luke calls, irritated. "We're safe in 'ere."

Both kids are still panicking, though, and Theo, Gabriela and Ashara are joining in. *What now?* Draining his glass, Luke turns to see Theo, through the kitchen doorway, holding a chair leg. The boy brings his bludgeon down to strike the floor, then recoils. Something small and brown scurries across the floor. *What the fuck?*

"Rats!" Evie shrills.

Rats? Luke grabs a wok from the drainer.

Chapter 65 — Naomi Adderley — 13:05

What a shithole.

Another town promoted from a village by the cotton and mining industries, Lowell is three quarters of the way from Wigton to Mortborough. It's been evacuated, but not quickly enough, judging by the dead bodies and crashed vehicles in the town centre. The smell of ash hangs in the air.

Naomi arrived five minutes ago, and she's already encountered the first zombies. She dodged them by sprinting through an outdoor market. *One good thing about these zombies — they're dumb as fuck.*

Café Napolitano sits across the road from the town hall, according to Panucci. His friend, who owns the coffee shop, is flouting the evacuation order. Aldo Baldini will supply the weapons and equipment Naomi needs. Once she's armed, she can continue her mission. Find Lena. *Get away from these godless freaks.*

Crouched behind a convertible sports car, she watches the café. No movement. A gunshot startles her and the pigeons thronging the town square. *Are those soldiers wearing black here too?*

Naomi takes one final look, both ways, down the high street. A lethargic zombie is just about in view to the right; it's not facing her way. She bolts across the road and down the alleyway to the left of Café Napolitano. As instructed by Panucci, she knocks on the side door three times. Footsteps sound inside.

But something's stirring in the skip at the end of the alley.

More footsteps in the building. Faint muttering.

Come on, Aldo

A hiss from the dumpster. When the shop's reinforced door opens, Naomi pushes her way inside, alarming the short, balding male on the other side.

"Alright, calm down!" the man protests, locking the door behind them.

Naomi apologises as her eyes adjust to the gloom: she's in a small commercial kitchen. The smell of freshly-brewed Americano is tantalising. On the hot plate, rather than dishes of food, there's a pistol, shotgun, ammunition and a rucksack. "Aldo, right?"

"Yeah. Naomi?"

"That's me."

"How are we lookin' out there?"

"Quiet. Couple of those freaks about, but not too many to dodge."

"Any military?"

"I heard gunfire."

"Wearin' black or camo?"

"Didn't see them." She nods at the equipment. "Is that mine?"

"Yup. Pep said you wouldn't need any tutorial on the weapons, but he did want me to show you this." From the bag Aldo takes a device that looks like a large smartphone. "Cellular networks are super-unreliable at the moment, but this uses satellites. Apart from connectivity, it works like any modern mobile. Pep said he wants you to ring him as soon as you arrive." He hands her the phone. "His and my numbers are the only ones in 'contacts'."

She dials for Panucci and waits a moment. Smiling, she accepts a mug of black coffee and a croissant. *Come on, Pep.*

"Hello, Nai?" Her friend sounds flustered.

"Pep? Everything okay?"

"Kinda. Just passed Wrexham. Traffic's still awful."

"Did you have any joy finding my friend?"

"Ya mean Lena? Don't worry. This line's secure. I've done a bit o' diggin' —"

"— And?"

"Ya know me. There's not a computer system in existence that I can't break. Hacked into her work email, her calendar. Her only upcomin' appointment was with a... Sofia Aslam, but in the 'comment' field, she's put 'CANCEL!!!' Three exclamation marks."

"She really didn't want to see Sofia Aslam, then."

"No. Which made me curious, so I logged into Aslam's account. Nothing suspicious there, but it took me to her personal email."

She taps her foot on the floor, eliciting a knowing smirk from Aldo. *Come on, Pep. Get to the point.* "So?"

"All of her personal emails were pretty dull." Panucci yawns for emphasis. "Except an exchange with a reporter, a Jada... Blacksack, Blaska... Bla-kow-ska, sorry. Long story short, looks like Lena's employee, Aslam, was gonna talk to the press."

"Probably something to do with all this shit that's been happening. But even if it is, where does it leave us?"

"Good question."

"Ugh! Pep, you're supposed to be helping me."

Aldo chuckles, but stops at a bump on the door.

"I'm tryin'! But I've only had a couple of hours."

"Okay, sorry." Naomi takes a deep breath. "Are there any phone numbers in the emails or calendar. You know, like in the 'contact info'."

"No, but there's an email to Blaska... Blaksa —"

"— Jada."

"Yeah. To Jada, from a Gracie McCall, who says she's got a new phone number. Sounds like she works for one of the big online media sites, HotTake. I'll forward it to you."

Another clang on the steel fire exit has Aldo on the move. He grabs a meat cleaver, tiptoes across the kitchen and peers through a spyhole. "Shit. Two of 'em." He pulls a silver revolver from his belt.

Jada frowns. "Forward all the emails to me, please. I better get out of here. Bell me if you find anything else."

"Will do." Panucci clicks his tongue. "You should have those emails by now."

"Great. And thanks, Pep."

"No problem. Listen, it's dangerous out there. I would tell ya to hole up with Aldo, but I know what yer like when you've got yer mind set on somethin'. So take care, okay?"

"Yeah, you too." Naomi ends the call and sees Aldo, still at the door, watching through the peephole. "Why don't you come with me, Aldo? There are vehicles we could take."

"No, thanks." He turns and puffs out his chest. "I inherited this place from my papa, God rest his soul. If he knew I just abandoned it, he'd turn in his grave."

After thanking Aldo, Naomi sneaks out of the café's front door. She immediately hears the scrape of shoes on tarmac. *Must be the ones who were at Aldo's side door.* Squinting against the sun, she jogs back to her bike, which is parked at the bus station. Footsteps follow. She increases her pace without looking over her shoulder and leaves her pursuers behind, dodging stalled cars, then buses. For a brief, chastening moment, her heart is in her mouth. The motorcycle isn't where she left it. Then she realises and curses herself: the bus terminal is symmetrical, and she arrived at the opposite end. Sure enough, the Honda's on the other side, gleaming.

Climbing on, she keeps an eye on her surroundings. There's a stray dog sniffing at some overturned bins, but it pays her no notice. The ticket office is empty, its glass front shattered. A single double decker bus is at Stop H. No one is aboard, unless they're hiding. Naomi fishes in the rucksack, retrieves the satellite phone and calls Gracie McCall. She holds her breath. Twenty seconds pass. The call goes to a voicemail service, with which she leaves a vague yet urgent message requesting a call back.

I desperately need her to ring me back. Otherwise, what am I doing next? Riding to Mortborough, to Evolve HQ? To do what?

Of course, she muses as she starts the bike's engine, Panucci could find something more concrete.

If he doesn't, though, and McCall doesn't ring me back — she might be dead herself — then I'm screwed. Or rather, Lena's screwed.

She kicks the stand and twists the throttle. Unsurprisingly, the noise draws attention, and half a dozen zombies are shambling her way before she's even left the terminus. But she's too fast. Roaring onto the main road from Lowell to Mortborough, she savours the wind in her hair for all of fifteen seconds before she hears a ringtone from her bag. Naomi pulls over with a screech, turns off the ignition and answers the call. "Yes?" Her eyes flicker from car to semi-detached house, in case her pause has caught the notice of any local monsters.

"Hello. Who is this?" The accent is middle class English.

"Naomi Adderley. Is that Gracie McCall?"

"Why d'you want to know?"

"I'm looking for my sister —"

"— Lena Adderley. Yes, I know who she is. But what d'you want from *me?*"

Naomi gives a brief explanation of Panucci's detective work.

McCall is silent for so long that Naomi checks to ensure the call's still connected. "So you're here to clean up your sister's mess?"

"What? No, I just want to make sure she's okay. I've not been able to reach her."

"So your family's reputation —"

"— Means nothing to me right now. I need to make sure Lena's safe. That's all I care about."

"I don't know where Jada is. Hopefully, she's okay. She never mentioned your sister, only the Evolve scientist she was interviewing. So I can't be of much assistance, I'm afraid. I've got a few useful contacts, and I'm trying to find Jada, but I've not had any luck so far. I'll get back to you if I hit on anything. As long as you do the same if you hear anything."

"Of course." Naomi deflates. *Another dead end. But what did I expect? Why did I think some woman Lena's presumably never met could help? I'm getting desperate. That's why.* "Hopefully they'll both be okay. Thanks for calling back, anyway."

"Sure. One thing I will say is this. Stay away from Mortborough. If your sister's there, she's already dead. Same goes for Jada. I'm lucky. I left Manchester as soon as I heard about the... disturbances. Somehow, I just knew it had something to do with what Jada was investigating." McCall clears her throat. "I'm in Scotland now. Though I'd love you to find your sister and my friend, I don't think you've got much of a shot."

"I know. It's... a stab in the dark, to put it mildly."

159

"Very mildly, from what I've heard. So, to be honest, I suggest you get as far away as you can."

"Okay, thanks for the advice."

Advice I can't take. She says goodbye, then restarts the Honda. A dead elderly couple stumble down their driveway, arms outstretched, so Naomi rides on. *If I do as McCall says, I'll be giving up on my own flesh and blood.*

Before long, she sees smoke on the horizon. There are multiple plumes, like she's nearing a war zone. The pitter-patter of automatic rifle fire is punctuated by the less frequent boom of heavier ordnance. A sign on Manchester Road tells Naomi she's a mile from Mortborough as she spots the first aircraft. *Machine gun drones, Panucci said. And there's so many of them…*

They can't all be armed? That much firepower would surely have won the battle by now.

Some of the houses on either side of the A-road are scorched black; many have shattered windows. Her speed reduces due to the increased number of abandoned cars and vans, and she has to meander between patches of broken glass. Twice she rolls through dark red spills, leaving bloody tyres tracks in her wake. Undead residents appear at doorways on three occasions. Their faces are glimpsed for no more than a heartbeat, but their contorted features, gaping wounds and haunted expressions won't be forgotten any time soon.

Thirty seconds later, she reaches a roadblock of sandbags topped by barbed wire. She could climb over, but then she would be forced to leave behind the motorbike. So she turns down a sidestreet, hoping for a detour. The B road running parallel with Manchester Road is similarly obstructed, as are all the others Naomi tries. *Completely cut-off.*

Therefore, Miss Adderley has a decision to make.

She can head into the eye of the storm, Mortborough, on foot. Pros: she'll be in the environs of her sister's place of work; she knows the area well. Cons: she'll have no transport; she has no idea whether Lena is anywhere near Evolve HQ; the town looks like London during the Blitz – if the invaders were undead, and the Stukas were gun drones.

Or Naomi can skirt Mortborough, make it her final destination, her last resort. Pros: less chance of being shot by flying machines or eaten by bloodthirsty cannibals; she can retain the motorcycle; the delay will give Pepe and McCall more time to obtain intel. Cons: she might be leaving her older sibling to die; she'll have to wait to play with the new toys Aldo gave her.

Come on, Nai. Now's not the time to develop an indecisive streak. What would Dad do? Nothing at the moment, for his dementia has scraped out his core and left a shell of the dynamic man who became a millionaire in his twenties.

What would Dad have done at my age, though? She doesn't know. Perhaps her apple fell further from his tree than she likes to think.

Naomi makes a conscious effort to slow her breathing. Once upon a time, she laughed at the concept of 'mindfulness'. As she's matured, however, she's learnt its benefits. So, staring at the winding trail of razor wire atop this Kenworthy Street's barricade, she focuses on the sun's rays on her skin, the breeze in her feathery hair, the stench of smouldering ruins, the taste of dust, the whirring of a motor.

Wait... a motor? That's not a good thing. Twisting left, right, and one hundred and eighty degrees, she sees nothing of significance. Then she looks up.

The descending UAV looks almost alien, but the cannon under its body is real enough.

Chapter 66 — Jada Blakowska — 13:35

They've turned a corner now, figuratively speaking. Her idea of distracting the undead around the tram with a grenade worked better than she could've dreamed. The pharmacy yielded nothing but fire and smoke, before the zombies nearby chased the survivors into a diner, wasting valuable time. Yet, before despondency could return, a drone attacked the hungry freaks, allowing their quarry to escape. Two streets later, Jada and her comrades hit the jackpot.

An ambulance. Its front end crumpled into a war memorial, poppy wreaths scattered across its fractured windscreen. Back doors yawning, an empty, blood-soiled stretcher half onboard, half on the pavement. And, most crucially, the vehicle contained a plethora of medical supplies.

Before they departed, Ashara gave them a list of the equipment and medications necessary to treat Lena. Now they have everything they need. Within half an hour, they'll have the Evolve CEO hooked up to a drip, flushing the poison from her veins. And her truth will flush the poison from the Government.

Nice metaphor, Jada. You can include it in your bombshell article, no, your book… *if you get away from the hundreds o' zombs, soldiers an' drones infestin' Manchester, that is.*

They can't get ahead of themselves. Because, at the moment, they're still in Salton Quays. Once they'd taken the medicines, they were forced away from the cenotaph and down a blind alley next to a convenience store. Using their rifles, they slew the zombies giving chase, took cover behind a pair of recycling bins and prayed their gunfire wouldn't summon unwanted attention. Twice the trio have tried to rejoin the main road. On both occasions, the presence of drones has compelled them to wait.

Brad brandishes the bag of meds. "What good's all this shit if we're stuck down 'ere? Lena's gonna die while we're shittin' ourselves in a corner."

"Lena'll die if we get smoked on da way back," Floyd reiterates. "An' I don't know 'bout you, but I don't plan on dyin' to save some rich bitch, ya get me?"

"It's not just about savin' her life, though, is it?" Jada risks a look past the cardboard/paper canister. There's nothing to see besides the rear wheels of the ambulance and the glass office building opposite the late shop. "It's about —"

"— Justice, exposin' da politicians. Yeah, you already said all dat. Jus' give it another five minutes. If nuttin' comes, den we'll have another look."

Brad huffs but holds his tongue.

"Hang on a minute." Again Jada leans out into the open. "That glass buildin'... it's a pretty good mirror if ya get the right angle." She shifts her position marginally, squints as reflected sunlight dazzles her, shuffles further to the right. "There we go!"

"What?" Brad hunkers down behind her. "Shit, yeah! That's cool. Is that…"

Jada gasps as her collar tightens; Floyd's yanking both of his friends back into the shadows. "Hey! Take it easy, Floyd —"

The whine of a passing UAV silences her and Brad. Thirty seconds later, they try again. This time the way is clear for long enough to satisfy Private Nelson, who leads them to the end of the passageway. They dash halfway across the road and stop at the memorial. Two drones are to their left, hovering twenty feet in the air, facing in the opposite direction. So they go right. Crawford Road is a dual carriageway, with plenty of stationary vehicles, tram stops, exchange boxes and advertising panels to use as cover.

Floyd is their eyes and ears, having the uncanny ability to advance swiftly whilst checking corners, scanning the road ahead and keeping an eye on the sky.

"Down behind dat cop van!" he hisses as they pass the entrance to a grand international hotel.

Instantly, Jada and Brad comply.

"Four tangos, twelve o'clock." Floyd grits his teeth. "Behind dat bus."

"Zombs?" asks Brad.

"Yeah. We can shoot dem, but be better if we don't. Too many nosey drones about, listenin'."

Glad of the chance for rest yet frustrated by the halt in progress, Jada uses the heel of her hand to clear sweat from her eyes. *We could go through the hotel. It overlooks the dockside, so we can follow the water. But if there are bad guys down there, we'll be stuck.* She turns away from the modern edifice to see the central reservation. Dividing one side of the carriageway from the other, it's short enough to jump. "Come on. Over that." She points.

Floyd grimaces. "We don't know what's on da other side, dough."

There's a clatter from the other side of the police van, then heavy footsteps. Glass crunching underfoot.

"Fuck it." Floyd runs and hurdles the hedge.

As do Jada and Brad. The eastbound half of Crawford Road is as congested by empty vehicles as its reverse, but there's no sign of enemy movement.

Until they stumble upon three zombies behind a set of roadworks. The fiends are on all fours on the asphalt, their faces buried in the remains of an obese man, so they were obscured till it was almost too late. Heart hammering in her ears, Jada backs away from the gruesome scene and hides with her friends behind a bus shelter. Luckily, the zombs are too engrossed by their entrée to realise they missed out on a main course.

Floyd leads them off the road proper. They cut across a petrol station forecourt in order to avoid the feasting monsters.

The next handful of undead are trying to break into a car. Presumably, the dead driver, still holding the steering wheel, has piqued their interest. At this point, the pavement runs parallel with an office block, so the survivors have to jump the central hedge onto the westbound lane.

They've travelled two hundred yards in this manner when the radio buzzes. Crouching behind an overturned Royal Mail van, wrinkling her nose at the tang of engine oil, Jada answers. "Luke? Do you read me? Over."

"Yeah, loud 'n' clear." He sounds ruffled. "Bit of a problem 'ere. We got - attackin' - the flat. Over."

"You got *what*?" Brad asks. "Over."

"Rats. Zombie-fuckin'-rats, comin' through the walls, floors, ceilin'..."

"Shit." Jada shares a worried look with Brad; Floyd's keeping watch on the road behind and ahead. "Just hang on. We got the meds. Be back ASAP. Over."

"That's another -. Lena's -. Don't know how long she's - left. Can you - - me? O-."

"Not very well," says Brad. "We'll be —"

The volley of machine gun fire has Jada's guts in turmoil. At least forty rounds are fired in a three second stretch. A quarter find the delivery truck. Like heavy rain on a tin roof. Most of the lead misses, however, hitting cars to the east instead. Windscreens explode; tyres burst; bodywork is riddled.

Brad's covering his ears against the din. "What're they shootin' at?"

Using his rifle scope, Floyd studies the vehicles already passed. "I'm not sure… wait! MIBs."

"Musta been followin' us," Jada says.

"What now?" Brad wonders. "Stuck between a rock 'n' an 'ard place, 'ere."

Another ripple of fire is rewarded by a cry of pain.

Floyd purses his lips. "Must be regular Army takin' 'em on."

Bullets whistle westwards; the men in black are fighting back.

Jada cringes. "We're really, really exposed here…"

"I don't think the MIBs wanna get us, though," Brad muses. "They've been trailin' us. Woulda killed us by now."

Still, we need to get outta here. The mail van rests partly on the pavement separating Crawford Road from a budget hotel. Beyond bloodstained revolving doors, the lobby is a nightmarish movie set. Corpses are slumped across leather sofas and chairs; arterial arcs decorate the walls. "Cut through there?" Jada suggests. "It'll have a terrace overlookin' the water..."

"Good finkin'." Floyd takes a final peek through his rifle scope. "MIBs pinned down. Let's go." Keeping low, the AWOL soldier makes his move.

Jada and Brad are hot on his heels. As the former crosses the sidewalk, she glances to her right – a camouflaged APC is flanked by at least a dozen British Army troops, two of whom point and shout – and to her left – one paramilitary in black is squatting behind a bullet-holed hatchback. Shots are loosed. The hotel doors disintegrate into cubes of jagged ice. Concrete chips erupt from the ground. The wind of a passing slug caresses Jada's hair.

And then they're inside.

"Keep goin'!" Floyd roars.

Jada dodges a dumb waiter. Slides in pooling blood. Hears a stirring from the lounge, unsteady footsteps, a television playing for no one. Into a kitchen. A giant male in chef's whites half-dyed red blocks the way; Floyd lands a headshot on the run. An undead female member of staff appears from behind a fridge; Brad and Jada blow the creature to oblivion. Out of the kitchen, into a gloomy corridor. Already reaching its end, Floyd kicks open a fire exit. Sunlight beckons. The sound of gulls.

Out on the terrace, they pass plastic tables still laden by half-empty glasses. There are three bodies on the ground; one stirs, but Floyd's rifle stops it for good. Over a low wall they climb. The dock's waters, dappled by sun rays, shift in the breeze.

"Okay, don't fink we're bein' followed." Floyd turns right, and the three slow to a trot as they follow the edge of the basin.

The skirmish on Crawford Road is stuttering to a conclusion. After a couple of grenade blasts and a final crescendo of automatic fire, relative silence reigns. The noise of distant battles has become so ubiquitous that Jada barely notices its rumble.

"D'ya think they'll follow us?" Brad says. "The proper army, I mean."

"Dunno," replies Floyd. "But we'll carry on as if dey are."

Shielding her eyes from the sun, Jada can just about see their destination: Ramona Quay. Its antiquated docking cranes are a five minute jog from the canal tunnel the crew passed earlier. The path is clear. There are no zombies lurking. No gunmen lying in wait. Of course, they have to be cautious of the buildings on their right, which could conceal any number of threats, but at least they only have to look one way, for the water to their left holds no surprises. Also, the skies have been free of drones for at least ten minutes.

The walkway ends in the shadow of the blue steel cranes. Standing guard over the Manchester Ship Canal, the rusty structures are planted in an acre of open land bordered by a car park. Several vehicles lie dormant; all are empty. *Except… is there someone in that white van? No, just my tired eyes.*

Indefatigable, Private Nelson crosses the parking lot. Jada and Brad are close behind, their eyes intent on the junction of Crawford Road and Monarch Road. There's nothing to see, though. Perhaps the Army, having defeated their black-wearing counterparts, have moved on to threats bigger than one deserter and two random citizens.

Just another half an hour, now, an' we can have a break. Once we've taken care o' those rats. Jada shakes her head at the thought of rodents terrorising her friends.

"Freeze! Don't move a fuckin' muscle!" The man's accent is local, his voice familiar.

Brad's neck twitches, but a gunshot keeps him staring straight ahead.

"I said, 'don't move'! You fuckin' retarded, or somethin'?"

Who is that? He sounds like…

"What do ya want?" Floyd's forearms are taut.

"Drop yer weapons, all o' ya. *Now*!"

Jada is first to comply. For a moment, she fears one of her companions will resist. But both men see sense and toss their rifles to the ground.

Multiple footsteps are getting closer. Though desperate to turn on her heel and discover the identity of their foes, Jada maintains composure. She doesn't have long to wait, in any case. The individuals behind her are arcing their approach to pass their hostages. In her peripheral vision, she registers several men, all armed. Eventually, the eight males stand before her.

She knows only one of the thugs, and she knows him too well. "Danny? Danny Rowbottom!"

"That's me, darlin'." A shark's smile splits his cruelly handsome face. "Come t' save the day!"

Chapter 67 — Randall Maguire — 14:55

The Landcruiser's engine sputters to a stop. Bloody Barry Jones removes the keys, decamps and crouches to peer through the window of his open door.

Pulse quickening, Agent Randall Maguire keeps watch on the public house's entrance. The branches of twin fake palm trees sway in the wind. Numerous bodies – two sporting black fatigues, the rest in civilian wear – are on the gravel.

"Looks clear." Jones stands; Maguire joins him.

Together they inspect the corpses.

"Only the ones wearin' black 'ave bled more than a few splashes, see." Jones points. "So the rest were zombies when they got shot."

"Yeah." Maguire strokes his chin. "There's definitely been a battle o' some sort, hasn't there?"

Nodding, Jones approaches the pub. He stoops directly beneath the eaves of the roof and scoops up two shell casings. "Reckon these were fired on the roof. Rolled off an' landed 'ere."

"Probably." Maguire peers through a window to see upset tables and chairs, plus the remains of a door, over which a sign warns 'STAFF ONLY'. There's no movement inside, save the flutter of napkins on the bar as the breeze picks up.

They're at 'The Wharfstar', in Walkley. It's the last known location of Private Floyd Nelson, the deserter with an important prisoner. The young Grenadier Guarsdman holds in his hands a ticking timebomb of truth that, if detonated, could bring Westminster Palace crumbling to the ground. The fallout would be felt as far away as Guildford, Surrey, in the Maguire household. Briefly, images of his house trashed, his loved ones slaughtered flash across his mind's eye. *No. I won't let that happen. I* can't *let that happen. I* will *get the job done.*

He and Jones begin a search of the besieged tavern, which stinks of death. Dozens of zombies have been slain, particularly around the canal-facing bay window. The carnage is unimaginable, worse than anything they've encountered thus far. Blood, guts, bone. An intoxicating, multisensory cocktail that Maguire is eager to spit out. They go up to the accommodation quarters, clambering over the bodies clogging the stairway. A barricade of furniture at the entrance has been ripped to shreds. The first floor is otherwise bare, apart from empty bottles of water and mugs in the lounge they enter last. Only the attic above remains to be investigated, the entrance an open trapdoor in the kitchen.

A thud overhead chills Maguire's insides.

Pistol in one hand, Jones raises a forefinger to his lips. He creeps out of the living room. He's impressively stealthy for a big man.

Squeezing his own handgun tight, Randall tails his henchman into the hallway.

Once more, there's a thump. And now footfalls. Creaking floorboards inches above their heads. Going towards the kitchen.

The Welshman and the Irishman follow the treads deeper into the bowels of the apartment. Back into the kitchen, where the stench of death is most pungent. The hanging loft hatch is now swaying slightly, and it's dripping blood.

Agent Maguire gulps. He wipes grime from his eyes with the back of his left hand.

A white mass falls from the loft and lands with a crash. Levelling their guns, Maguire and his escort wait for the humanoid figure to get up, but it doesn't move. Tentatively, Jones steps forward.

Bodies drop like a gory rockfall: four, five, six. *What the fuck?*

Both men are still as stone. Watching, ready, they train their weapons on the heap of inhumanity beneath the attic door.

Clothes rustle. The linoleum floor squeaks. Then two of the cadavers come back to life, casting their inanimate cousins aside as they rise.

Firing simultaneously, Jones and Maguire fill the hunks of decomposing meat with lead. The former aims a foot higher, tattooing his crewcutted mark's face, painting the head height cupboards behind with vital fluid and brain matter. The latter's rounds strike centre mass, as he was taught in academy. But his training is not appropriate to today's scenario. Forward stumbles the female zombie, dark fingers pincering, spectacled eyes bulging, frizzy hair bouncing, bleeding from its breasts.

Jones switches his aim and shoots just as Maguire corrects his own line of fire.

Shot either side of its nose, the beast sinks to the ground.

Ears ringing, Maguire exhales. Too early, he realises, as an iron grip finds his right ankle. One of the fallen bodies, its legs mangled, is crawling. As he topples, the agent hears two Glock blasts. The hand grasping his leg relinquishes its hold. "Thank you." He accepts Bloody's hand and regains his feet.

"No problem, sir." Jones reloads his gun.

They clear the pub without finding Nelson or Adderley's bodies, and move on to the beer garden by the canal. Several MIB corpses are found. Some have bullet wounds; others were killed by cannibals.

Scrutinising the mud underfoot, Jones opens the gate at the rear. "Footprints, sir. Leadin' onto the towpath."

Maguire stares at the waterway, almost transfixed by the undulating, shimmering surface. "Ya reckon they took a boat?"

"Looks that way, it does. Trail ends right at the edge." The gangling aide looks both ways and shrugs. "There's no way o' knowin' which way they went, is there?"

"No. But, Adderley came from Mortborough. It's unlikely they'd head back that way, innit? Goin' back into the eye of the storm doesn't make sense."

"I suppose so. We go left, then?"

"Yeah." Now Maguire goes first. Although only intuition is driving him eastwards, his conviction is strong. *What if I'm wrong, though? Fifty-fifty chance that could lead to a terrifyin' end for Caylie an' Ronan.* "There's a barge." He points at a watercraft painted red, white and blue.

"'The Sharpest Fang', it's called."

"Funny name for a pleasure boat. Come on. Let's get onboard. Hopefully, it has keys in the ignition."

It doesn't, but that proves no problem for Jones, who's able to hotwire it into life. The engine chugs lethargically. Even at maximum output, their speed is limited to six knots, when they're not steering past floating bodies, submerged cars and idle craft.

Maguire pilots. The scuffle in the pub left him listless and sluggish; now, at the helm of 'The Sharpest Fang', with a cool breeze offsetting the blazing sun, despite the sickly-sweet smell of corruption in the air, he's reinvigorated. He ignores the nagging doubt in his head. The voice whispers that he chose the wrong direction, that they should be travelling west, that he was simply too afraid to go to Mortborough, the town of the dead, that he's sacrificing his family out of fear. *This is the right way. I think so. Jones thinks so.*

Correct choice or not, their current transport is too slow. Therefore, when they chance upon a police boat, they pull alongside and transfer from one watercraft to the other. Maguire almost falls in the water. Jones laughs. Then apologises.

There's a dead constable on the floor of the boat. Randall feels hollowness instead of revulsion; he's becoming desensitised already. With some difficulty, the pair heave the heavily-built officer into the water and continue downstream. The emergency service vehicle is markedly faster than the barge. As their progress quickens, Agent Maguire's spirits soar. A break from killing reincarnated civilians-turned-demons helps, too, and he barely notices the bloated corpses bobbing in the water.

The human buoys soon become too commonplace to disregard. Eventually, the two government men reach a wooded spot where the canal is partially blocked by dead people. There's enough space through which to squeeze, but the presence of another boat causes Maguire to pause.

"Ya think that's Nelson's ride?" asks his underling.

"Could be." *We don't even know for definite that he took a boat.* He shakes his head to expel the misgiving. *It's all we have to go on, for now.* "Why would they stop 'ere?"

"Beats me. Perhaps the canal was blocked worse when they got 'ere."

"How would it unblock, though? Oh, yeah. Some o' the bodies could've come back to life. Let's check the bank."

The section of path closest to the abandoned boat is covered in dried mud. There's far more than one would expect from one wayward soldier and his CEO prisoner, but if Jones has indeed guessed shrewdly, the excess traffic would be due to undead climbing out of the water, perhaps in pursuit of Nelson… *Lotta ifs, buts an' maybes, right enough.*

Barry runs a hand through coal black hair. "We'll check the boat, sir? Could give us some clues."

"Good thinkin'." Maguire bites his lip; he doesn't dare hope for a positive sign. *What if we find nothin'? Is an empty vessel and a load o' mud enough to justify gettin' out here?*

The duo disembark. As Jones steps onto the other craft, his boss makes a decision. If there's no proof of Nelson utilising the boat, he'll contact Headquarters and ask for more support. While they're unlikely to send troops or armed UAVs, it might be worth a try. When Maguire checked in earlier, during the drive from the farm, HQ agreed to spare a technician to check local CCTV and drone footage. Said staffer is yet to provide results.

"Can't see anything, sir." Bloody's eyes are busy, but there's nothing to see. "Muddy footprints, large ones —"

"— The private's not far off two metres tall —"

"— Yeah, but apart from that…"

"Lemme have a look." Maguire boards the moored craft. *Steering wheel, acceleration lever thing, life-jackets. All pretty standard. Hold up…*

On the glass of the windshield, there are several fingerprints. Pulling his smartphone from his pocket, the agent feels his own heartbeat in his ears. His palms are sweaty, his knees weak, as he logs in to a seldom used phone application. He presses the camera icon. Focusses on the largest of the prints. Clicks once, hears the shutter sound. And waits.

Arms folded, Jones keeps an eye on the woods to their rear. "Nice toy, sir."

'NO MATCH', the app states.

Shit. "I'll try a couple more." Again he opts for the larger latents, again without luck.

"Maybe he had gloves on, sir? Or maybe he just wasn't 'ere."

I'll try one more. Inexplicably, he's drawn to a smaller imprint. *Could've been his little finger…*

'MATCH FOUND'.

A cog turns on the screen, and Maguire's stomach performs a similar manoeuvre.

'PRIVATE FLOYD NELSON, GREN GDS…'

Throbbing with adrenaline, the agent stares at the soldier's photograph. He's already read the man's profile, but he does so again. The young man has no spouse, no known dependents. Murdering him will be immoral nonetheless, but Maguire can't afford to be sentimental. *Nelson's life for Caylie's and Ronan's. A trade I'd make every day o' the week. Shit, I'd nuke the whole country if I had to.*

"Result, sir?" Jones, now holding his assault rifle, seems distracted.

"Yeah. We'll follow the tracks into the woods."

"Maybe not right away."

The agent frowns. "What's wrong?"

"We're bein' watched. In the trees. Men-in-black. Just stay still, sir."

Cursing his luck, Maguire does as advised. He scans the forest, sees nothing but dry vegetation, glances at his protector, and shrugs. "I don't see 'em."

"I'm gonna count to three. When I fire, you jump out an' get behind that big oak. The one with a love-heart carved into it. Okay, sir?"

"Okay."

"One. Two. Three." Jones brings his longarm to bear in a flash; Maguire vaults over the side of the boat as the first shots ring out. He feels the passage of a bullet as he goes.

Need to stay alive. Can't die now.

Because if he's killed, Caylie and Ronan will be next.

Chapter 68 — Luke Norman — 14:45

He stomps. The tiny vermin underfoot squirms for the briefest moment, but it becomes limp when he bears down. *Jesus, this is grim.*

There's a crack to his right: Ashara, wielding a saucepan, has just crushed a rat against the bathroom tiles. Dark fluid fills the grout as she raises the pan again. Luke doesn't watch; he hears claws on the floor behind the toilet bowl. As soon as the dark brown critter appears, he brings his heel down on its back. Small bones break.

Someone screeches in another room. *Living room?* Grabbing his wok, Luke leaves Ashara in the bathroom. Out into the short corridor. The light bulb's flickering, ready to blow. In the corner of his eye: movement? Or his mind playing tricks? Another scream. Glass smashes. A thud, tumble, somebody grunting in pain.

Now he's in the lounge. Warmer. Smells of grimy bodies. It's dark, the only source of illumination the gap between the curtains. Barely three seconds after the first shout. Feels like an age. *Why's the light off?* People are moving, whimpering. He hears Connor. *Can't see a fuckin' thing!* Heading for the window, he stands on something small. *A rat?* No – Evie yelps.

His shin erupts in pain as he blunders into something solid. "Fuck!" Limping now, Luke reaches the sliver of sunlight. He seizes a drape, yanks it wide open. Harsh light momentarily blinds him. But when he turns away from the window, he can see. Evie's on the ground. A rat's at her shoe, chewing on leather. Theo's on his knees; blood drips from his face. Gabriela's using a table leg to whack something on the ground by the TV.

Where the fuck is Connor?

The kitchen. On the way, Luke stands on the zomb-animal attacking Evie. He twists his foot, feels a crack and hurdles the coffee table that almost broke his tibia. Boots a ball of fur, teeth and claws scurrying towards Theo. And opens the kitchen door.

Flat on his back, Connor is sobbing.

Gould's on top of him. "Come here, you little shits!" the transport employee spits. He pulls away from the boy with a rodent tail in each hand. The two mini-monsters squirm in his grasp, desperate to bite his arms. He swings them both simultaneously against the wall. There's a sound like water balloons bursting as dark smears appear on the wallpaper. One of the kids in the living room cries out, so Gould goes to help.

Connor's getting to his feet. Something's moving behind him, however. At the angle of kitchen counter and plasterboard, an especially rotund rat is struggling to squeeze through the hole in the wall used by its brethren.

Luke hefts his wok just as the beady-eyed horror pops onto the worktop. *'Ave some o' this!* He hacks down. His wrist pangs with the clanging impact. The undead animal dodged; he's missed. Again he readies to attack. But when he raises his arm once more, he finds he's only holding the pan handle. Its steel basin has broken off. So he jabs with the handle. This time he doesn't miss entirely, for the jagged edge pins a hindleg to the worktop. Squealing manically, the fat beastie twists and strains to free itself.

Connor grabs the detached wok basin and drops it over the stricken zomb-rat, trapping it inside. His father pulls the handle clear to create a seal. Underneath, the verminous prisoner rattles and scratches, moving the pan.

Muttering an expletive, Luke holds it still.

"What now?" his son asks.

"That carving knife, there. Pass it me. I'll lift the wok a tiny bit, 'n' stab the little bastard."

"No, it'll be too quick. Wait!" Connor opens the microwave oven at the end of the counter.

"Good thinkin', kid." Luke slides the upside down metal pot across the surface, positions it in front of the microwave, raises one side of the wok and lets the rat into the appliance. Before the varmint can realise its mistake, its foe slams shut the oven door. The rat squeaks and scrabbles; its protests go unheeded.

Luke breathes a sigh of relief. The apartment is relatively quiet, the threat overcome. He asks his child if he's alright, and the boy says he's fine. Heading back into the lounge, Luke hears beeping then a hum from his rear, but, suddenly weary, he dismisses the sound. Gould, Theo, Evie and Gabriela are sitting on the floor, nursing bruises and cuts. Ashara joins them, bloody saucepan in hand.

"We all okay?" the latter asks.

Everyone mumbles something in the affirmative as Luke sits on the sofa.

After a couple of minutes of silence, Gould stands, wincing. "Need to block up those holes. Look for any other weak spots in the walls.

Groaning inwardly, Luke nods. *I just wanna sit down 'n' close my eyes fer five minutes.* He knows Gould's right, though, so he gets up and goes to the kitchen. *What's that smell?* Then he sees the light. "What's that stink?"

"'S alright, Dad," Connor says. "Jus' the rat, in the microwave."

Luke pulls the plug from its socket. "Jeez, son, ya can't cook a live animal!"

"It's not alive. It's undead. Now it's dead again."

The youngster's right; the vermin's stopped scratching, and the stench of burning fur is sickening. *Is my kid a psychopath, or somethin'? No, he's jus' tryin' t' survive, like the rest of us.* Luke smiles at the boy, squeezes his shoulder and picks up the smoking, reeking microwave. He carries the appliance out of the apartment, down the corridor, to the stairwell, then dumps it on the landing.

Of course, the battle versus the crawling dead would've been easy had they been able to use firearms. But with troops still outside, they didn't want to draw attention with gunfire. *That's 'ow it's gonna 'ave t' be, at least till those soldiers 'ave fucked off.*

After re-entering the apartment, he locks the door behind himself. How long will they have to wait? he wonders. For that matter, how long will Lena last?

Shit! Lena! They've not checked on her. He dashes down the hallway. Piles into the bedroom. The Evolve chief is still in bed: motionless, pale, smelling sour. Unmolested thus far.

Claws on laminate floor. Yet Luke sees nothing. Sweating, he searches the room. He starts when the door creaks behind him, but it's only Gabriela.

"I only just remembered!" she pants. "Is she okay?"

"Yeah, but there's one in 'ere."

"A rat? Where?"

"Dunno. It's defo in 'ere, though. Can't you 'ear it?"

"No. I don't think so."

Eyes narrowing, Luke drops to the ground at least three feet from the bed. He doesn't want to get too close, in case the little pest jumps out and savages his face. He peers under the bed, cringing. *Shoulda brought a weapon, or somethin'*.

As if reading his mind, Gabriela hands him her table leg.

"Ta."

There's nothing under the bed, apart from a stray sock and a book. And with only a closet and bedside, there are no other hiding places in the bedroom... *I definitely 'eard claws, though. Didn't I?*

His ears were playing tricks on him, obviously. Overwrought and exhausted beyond belief, Mr Norman needs a rest. Gabriela volunteers to guard Lena, so he rejoins the others. They chat excitedly about the skirmish, but Luke's mind is wandering. He's daydreaming about his dad's place in the country, him walking hand-in-hand with Jada – *yeah, I know it's sad, but we do get on well, when we're not killin' undead* – with Connor riding his bike. No zombies. No MIBs. No drones. Dad would like Jada, too —

"Luke? Wake up, man!" Gould is pacing, agitated. "We need to get those holes plugged up."

"Okay, okay. Chill out." Reluctantly, he wrenches himself out of the gamer chair. "Best come up with a system for watchin' Lena, too. Can't just leave it all to Gabriela, can we?"

"No. Good thinking. I'll create a spreadsheet on the computer."

They devise a rota. Theo will relieve Gabriela after two hours, and he in turn will be replaced by Ashara. Gould will track CCTV feeds, while Connor periodically tries the radio and Evie keeps watch out of the window. Anyone not currently assigned a duty – Luke, Theo and Ashara – is to work on securing the apartment against any future rodent attacks. Formulating the plan expels Luke's fatigue, to a degree. At least they're not simply sitting around, waiting for Jada to return, or Lena to die.

They need to have a conversation about their next destination. Ashara took a turn on the computer and learnt the location of the refugee camp in Manchester that Gould mentioned. Luke favours using his father's house in the countryside as a hideout. The children are split. Connor and Gabriela prefer Luke's plan, while Theo and Evie endorse Ashara's.

Before the discussion can even begin, Gould catches Luke's eye. "I want a word, in private."

The younger man sighs inwardly. *This'll be fun.* "Sure. The kitchen, then?"

"No, the corridor outside."

Luke gives Ashara an apologetic shrug. Ridiculously, he feels nervous as he accompanies Josh out of the apartment, as though he's in trouble at school. He leans on the wall next to their flat's front door. "What's up?"

"We need to get out." The bus station supervisor's tone is casual, but the intensity in his eyes is disconcerting.

"I know. When Jada 'n' —"

"— No, now."

"Now? We've just come up with a rota, Josh. *Your* rota, your idea."

"Yes, but I've been thinkin' —"

"— What, over the last two minutes?"

"Yes. Well, no. It's been playing on my mind since before the rat invasion."

"What has?"

"There's a bus, just a couple hundred yards away. I spotted it on a CCTV feed. Looks like it's abandoned, the way it's been left, which means it probably still has keys in the ignition."

"A bus t' go where?"

"London."

Luke pushes himself away from the wall with a huff. "Fucksake, Josh. Not that again."

"Yes." Gould's nostrils flare. "*That* again. I'm sorry to inconvenience you with something as minor as truth, justice and the security of Great Britain and all her people, but —"

"— Christ, give it a rest. I know it's important the Government are exposed. But we're already workin' on it, remember. Floyd, Jada 'n' Brad are out there, riskin' their lives fer it, remember. We're 'ere, riskin' our lives t' protect Lena fer it, remember. What more d'ya want?"

"It's not enough, Luke! Jada, Brad, Floyd, they're going to die —"

"— They're *not* gonna die!"

"Yes, they will. And so will Lena. And by then, we'll have left it too late to get out. The military will probably just nuke the whole city. Then we'll be dead, and no one will ever know the truth, and millions more'll die because no one's being told the truth. No one's preparing."

"You don't know any of this!"

"I do. My friends have told me."

"Fer fucksake. We're not makin' decisions based on the voices in your fucked-up brain."

A muscle twitches in Gould's jaw, and his fists bunch. "It'll be on your head, then. When you die, when your boy dies —"

"— You fuckin' what?"

"You heard me."

Luke's vision wavers, becomes tinged red. He snatches the other man's collar. "Don't you fuckin' dare bring Connor into this. Don't you *fuckin'* dare, you prick!"

"Get your fucking hands of me!"

"Usin' my son's potential death t' try 'n' make a point? I should fuckin' knock you out, ya piece o' shit."

Gould clutches the fingers at his neck; his grip is uncommonly strong. He juts his forehead to within a millimetre of Luke's. "Just try it, wanker."

Headbutt the twat. Fuckin' break 'is nose. Talkin' 'bout my lad like that.

A tiny part of Luke recognises the foolishness of the set-to. They need to be united to survive; divided they will make easy pickings for the multitude of threats both inside and outside the tower. *But Gould's face is just beggin' for a smack...*

Chapter 69 — Naomi Adderley — 15:00

The bike idles, its frame throbbing between her legs. She could accelerate. She could use the Honda's raw power to get past the UAV. The Swinford avenue is almost clear of obstacles. There's a pothole in the centre of the road, a van half-parked on the pavement by the entrance to the park. *Nothing major.*

But she doesn't have to look far to find a reason to discourage said course of action. The evidence is there, right before her eyes, between her hands: scuffed paintwork on the handlebars from a cannon round. A millimetre lower, and the shot would've split the bars in two. At the speed she was travelling, she wouldn't have survived.

The first and only drone Naomi encountered, on the barricaded outskirts of Mortborough, almost killed her with a single burst of fire. She escaped with her life, though luck played a significant part. Presumably, the death-bot ran out of ammunition. Although it shadowed her for well over an hour while she wove and skidded around the streets of Presley Common and Ellandbrook, to the southwest of the roadblocks, it didn't rain lead on her again. Eventually, as she rode the back lanes past Walkley, her pursuer gave up its surveillance.

This new drone might not be as forgiving, however. Plus, it may have a full magazine of cannon shells, loaded and ready to make mincemeat of the youngest of the Adderley daughters. Presently, the pilot-less gunship is harmless enough. It's hovering above a warehouse, facing away from Naomi. Her bike is behind a pickup truck, so if the machine begins to turn, she can duck, and it won't see her.

I should just find another way past. Go left, and ride around the park. Or right, and through the industrial estate. It'll waste time, but I'm in no rush. I'm aimless, at the moment. Telling myself I'm not, that I'm taking action to save my sister. But really, what am I actually doing? I've been chased away from the only place I know where Lena might be. Not that it matters, because I was too scared to enter Mortborough anyway.

"What *are* you doing, Naomi?" she murmurs. "You're sitting there, watching a drone. Trying to ignore the smell of roasted meat coming from that old people's home on the next street. Jumping every time a gun fires somewhere. Practically shitting yourself whenever a bomb goes off." She inhales; the UAV's on the move again. It's going away, though, so she breathes out. "You're out of your depth, Nai. And now you're talking to yourself."

She needs inspiration, a lead to follow. A call from Panucci or McCall would be welcome, but both have been quiet.

Somewhere behind her a bottle rolls. Twisting in her seat, Naomi searches for the item in question. Was it blown over by the strengthening wind, or kicked by an unknown party? If it's a zombie stumbling around, perhaps in the building site to her rear, she has nothing to fear. The dead buffoons are no match for the motorcycle's speed and manoeuvrability. Living soldiers, whether uniformed in black or camouflage, are an entirely different proposition. Twice she's had to change route due to their attentions. The most recent close shave involved a single sharpshooter posted in Presley Common's church's bell tower. His – or her – first shot destroyed the Honda's right hand wing mirror. The second passed too close for comfort.

Again the bottle is disturbed. On this occasion, she sees the rolling article. It's to her right, at five o'clock, by a long-dilapidated public house. *That's a good sign, though, because there's no way trained troops would make the same mistake and betray their presence twice.* Naomi turns the handlebars to the left, her decision made. She'll keep the UAVs at arm's length. Take her chance with the undead instead. Maintaining a speed of twenty miles per hour, she skirts the park.

I'll head back to Mortborough. Try and get in from the north. Maybe use the motorway. There's more open land around there, so it'll be harder to barricade. With a bit of luck, I can stay on the bike —

The zombie practically leaps from behind the box van. More like a big cat than a former human, it lands right in front of her. Naomi reacts quickly, banking right. But she asks too much of the motorbike, which goes into a skid. *No no no. Don't fall off. Don't fall off.*

She barely keeps the vehicle upright. Skims a parked minibus. From behind that comes another dead walker. This one a woman in a burqa. Pulling hard left, she feels the Honda sliding beneath her. *If I hurt myself, crush my own leg, I'll be easy pickings.* With all her strength, she manages to avoid being unseated. Her equilibrium regained, she guns the engine and roars away.

I got complacent. Bike or no bike, I can't take the zombies lightly. Next time I won't be so lucky.

Miss Adderley brakes in the shadow of a warehouse and checks over her shoulder. Her ambushers are miniature now, plodding in pursuit, and the drone is out of sight. She continues until she reaches a junction that marks the northwest corner of the park. Turning left will take her back to Mortborough via Walkley; going right leads to Salton.

Come on, Nai. You've already decided. You're going back to your home town. Yeah, you're scared, and yeah, you probably won't make it out alive, but you can't leave Lena. What would Dad say if he knew you walked away now?

Grant Adderley might be dead already. If not, he could be in imminent danger, and with his progressive illness, he's more vulnerable than most. *Not that you'd know much about his dementia, Nai. You didn't even bother flying home when he was diagnosed.* Perhaps by saving him she'll be atoning for her neglect.

No. Dad would tell you to forget about him, and go for Lena.

So that's what she'll do. No more pontificating, no more procrastinating. Jaw set, she turns the front wheel of the Honda to the left, twists the throttle and —

The satellite phone's ringtone interrupts her moment of gritty resolve.

She hasn't saved the number yet, but she recognises the treble four digits at the end. Leaving the bike in the middle of road, she hides in a car and answers her mobile. "McCall?"

"Adderley. Where are you?" The editor sounds stressed.

"On my way to Mortborough. What's up?"

"Remember I said I have contacts?"

"Yeah?"

"Well, one of 'em, who shall remain unnamed, spends most of her free time listening to police radio traffic."

"I thought that was all encrypted now?"

"Not if you know what you're doing. Anyway." McCall says something intelligible to a third party. "The coppers are getting very frustrated."

Naomi puffs her cheeks. *Where is this going, exactly?* "Frustrated by what?"

"They've been evacuated from Greater Manchester, along with everyone else apart from the Army. But a local gangster, a thorn-in-their-side called Rowbottom, has been running amok. They have enough CCTV evidence to put him away forever, but they're being forced to sit on their hands by this lockdown."

"Okay. But what does this have to do with Lena and Jada?"

"This gang traffic drugs and people for a living. During all this chaos, they've been abducting young girls and women. Now, I'm guessing this sister of yours is a smart cookie, right?"

"Yeah."

"The city gets invaded by zombies, what's she likely to do?"

"Get out of there."

"Exactly." McCall continues: "Someone matching Jada's description has been spotted being followed by this gang."

A window smashed nearby; Naomi ducks to conceal herself. "So great. Sounds like we might be able to save your friend if we can find this Rowbottom character. But what about my sister?"

"Either she's escaped, or this gang have her."

"That's a helluva leap, McCall."

"It might be. But what else do you have to go on?"

"Not much. Where's this gang now?"

"Salton Quays."

They say their farewells, both women promising to notify the other should they make any further progress.

Naomi heads east, hating herself for the relief she feels at not having to go to Mortborough. *I'm basically being used. There's no evidence to suggest Lena's disappearance is related to Jada's. McCall knows I have nothing else to go on, and she's exploiting that, hoping I'll find her buddy.*

The sickening truth is that Gracie is right. While rescuing Blakowska is unlikely to further Naomi's cause, the alternative – searching the zombie, soldier and drone infested haystack of Mortborough for the needle also known as Lena – is even less feasible.

Riding past the park, slowly in order to keep the motorcycle's noise to a minimum, Naomi appreciates the disaster's full extent for the first time. A playground close to the perimeter has been devastated by fire, its climbing frame, slide and zip-line blackened, ash drifting on the breeze.

One hundred yards on, Naomi wishes she could smell burnt wood again. For the entrance closest to the botanical gardens is locked by a chain. Said obstruction is evidently responsible for the deaths of at least a dozen locals. *Probably more, because some will've turned into zombies.* Their scarlet-splashed corpses are gathered close to the gate, with two of the hapless deceased entangled in the fence. Arms and legs at crazy angles, mutilated faces clustered by flies, ripening in the sun. Vocal black birds scatter at the growl of Naomi's vehicle, only to return when she's passed by.

Football fields in the southeast corner have become battlefields strewn with bodies. Most are in civilian dress; many are in uniform; some are dismembered beyond recognition or cooked to a crisp. A tank, its hatch yawning, sits silent by a set of goalposts. Suddenly, the reek of smoke is back.

An A-road connects Swinford and Salton. It's a route Naomi took many times as a teenager, so as long as she's vigilant for enemies, she can travel on auto-pilot. She even takes the shortcut used by her younger self to avoid a typically-congested roundabout.

The diversion isn't necessary today, of course, but she's distracted by fears for her sister's doom and mental images of the diabolical scenes in the park. Now she realises her local knowledge is out of date, for Wendover Avenue has been cut in half by a walkway. *Probably something to do with that new school around the corner.* Railings prevent her from crossing. The Honda is marginally too wide to squeeze down the sides, thanks to bollards planted in the gaps. She has to double back.

When she turns she gasps. An undead male in the garb of an Orthodox Jew is at the end of a driveway to the right. Its arms and legs move spasmodically yet rapidly as it steps on to the pavement. A child zombie, coal-black pigtails bouncing, approaches from the left. *No probs, just two of them. They can choke on my dust.*

Except there aren't only two of them. Four more are en route, taking a left onto Wendover. Another three are coming from the opposite direction.

Shit. Back to the wall now. Nowhere to run.

Abandoning the bike is a solution, but without it Naomi's options are limited. Locating Rowbottom's gang would be nigh-on impossible. Fight or flight: she decides quickly. It's time to use the weapons sourced by Panucci. She hopes her hunting practice, honed in the USA, translates into effective survival skills.

Chapter 70 — Floyd Nelson — 15:20

If his trapezius muscles were any tighter, they would rupture. Because he's furious, consumed by a white-hot fire of anger being stoked by every gun muzzle prod and every insult. His best friend is dead. His Army career over. The people responsible will never meet justice. Thousands of ordinary folk have died. Millions more could soon follow them to the grave. Or worse, condemned to an afterlife as a freak of nature hungry for human flesh.

And, to put the glaze on the cherry on the icing on top of the cake, Floyd and his friends have been abducted by a bunch of chavs. As cowardly as they are ill-mannered, the Mancunian lowlifes wouldn't dare face him in a fair fight. They had to take him unawares. *Attackin' from behind like little bitches.* They're stupid, too, not realising they wouldn't have enough room in the van for the eight of them plus their prisoners. Which means the three survivors are being escorted through Salton at gunpoint. On foot.

Strangely enough, they're bearing towards Churchill Heights. As yet, they've not been robbed – apart from having the radio taken when it betrayed its own presence by crackling – so the medical supplies have not been stolen. Nor have they been harmed. *What dey want from us?* Theo told of his narrow escape from these criminals; he and Gabriela mentioned a rumour about Rowbottom abducting young women.

So is it just Jada dey want? If she's the only captive of value, Floyd and Brad are expendable. The journalist will suffer, but she might escape or be freed. Her male friends won't live to see any such reprieve.

The thug ushering him backs off a little to talk to an associate, giving Floyd the chance to take in his surroundings. Concrete tenement flats, neglected houses and graffiti'd, long-closed shops remind him of his youth. He recalls the hoodlums on street corners, their dress not dissimilar to that of Rowbottom and his cronies. The smell of marijuana, the occasional tinkle of breaking glass, the taste of cheap vodka his mates pressured him to try. Sunny afternoons like today's meant the females would wear skimpier clothes to attract the players with the most clout. Floyd pretended to find them alluring, when it was the scowling, posturing drug dealers who appealed to him.

His mother strove to discourage him from the street. In truth, he didn't need much guidance. The likes of Rando and Durrell G were handsome and charismatic, but their vicious, callous natures were self-evident. Plus, many wound up dead or in jail. In fact, a couple of the more psychopathic – Lenny Smith and C-Dog, if he remembers correctly – were implicated in a scheme not unlike Rowbottom's. Getting vulnerable girls addicted to drugs, detaining them in squalid conditions then profiting from their bodies, the degenerates eventually met justice, but not before they murdered one of their slaves' brothers, a twelve year-old who was kidnapped along with his fourteen year-old sibling.

Dat'll be me 'n' Brad. Collateral damage like young Marvin McGee. Shot in da face cos he wasn't any use to da bastards.

"Hold up!" Rowbottom, at the front of the convoy, has a deeper voice than the rest. He's the alpha of this pack of mangy wolves.

Everyone stops.

Nelson winces as a pistol barrel jabs his lower back.

"Don't go gettin' any ideas, soldier-boy," growls the diminutive, sallow-faced goon assigned to Floyd. "Get down."

Staring straight ahead as though he's on the parade ground, the prisoner drops to his haunches but says nothing in reply.

Ten yards in front, Rowbottom is crouching behind a roadside skip.

"He knows his shit." The short gangster copies his leader will taking cover. "Danny's like a commando, or somefin'."

"He wasn't like a commando earlier, was he?" Floyd jibes.

"What ya mean?" the ruffian asks.

"Dat tower. In Walkley. Orion flats, I fink dey call it. His buddies got smoked."

"That was just a loada kids. He's got us down with 'im now." The man flourishes his pistol, which looks like an Army issue. "'N' we all tooled-up, bro."

"Shut the fuck up, Gibbo," Nidge, Rowbottom's closest lieutenant hisses. "We got mongs up 'ere."

'Mongs'? Is dat what dey call da zombies?

If so, it's the second time the unlikely group has encountered the undead. On the first occasion, they were on the edge of the Quays when six dead hotel staff ambushed them. The gangsters acted tough afterwards, boasting about their exploits, but they were undisciplined and disordered during the battle.

Floyd cranes his neck to see past a filthy caravan. *More dan 'alf a dozen dis time.* Ten foes await. No, eleven. A baby, its dimpled cheeks flecked scarlet, grips the bars of a play-pen on an overgrown lawn. The monsters are in the garden of a larger, older house, a corner-plot. They're gathered around a barbecue. While some sport tracksuits like Rowbottom's followers, others are dressed for summer: in flip-flops, vests and shorts. Crushed beer cans and cigarette butts litter the patio. Most of the plastic furniture is spattered with blood. A disembowelled cat floats in a paddling pool.

Cut down dat ginnel dere. Go 'round dem, not right past dem. Nuttin' to be gained from beefin' wid dese ugly fucks. Floyd's not in charge of tactics, however.

Daniel 'Pimp Daddy' Rowbottom is calling the shots, and it seems he's emboldened by his victory against the hotelier zombs. Misappropriated assault rifle ready, he turns to face his mob. "Right. 'Ere's what's goin' down. We ain't fuckin' about. We walk right up t' these cunts, 'n' we fuck 'em up."

His underlings nod. There's doubt in their eyes, though.

"We got the weapons. They're jus' fuckin' mongs, remember. Gibbo, you stay 'ere wi' these dickheads. Any of 'em move, ya blow 'em away. Ya get me?"

"Fuck yeah, Danny." Gibbo chambers a round in his pistol.

Rowbottom hefts his machine gun. He revels in the adulation of his men for a moment, cherishing their devotion. Yet he's in no rush. *Dat motherfucker's shittin' his pants. He can't back down, dough. Not now, not in front of his boys.*

After an awkwardly-long pause, the felon rounds the skip and strides towards the enemy.

"Come on," says Gibbo. "Behind that skip. We'll 'ave a better view." The temporary gaoler waves his handgun, and his detainees trudge towards the yellow-and-black container, which is by the pavement on the opposite side of the road to the patio of the dead.

Resting his arms on the skip's rusty ledge, Floyd watches events unfold.

Rowbottom fires from the hip but doesn't hit anything. "Come on, then!" he roars, as if challenging a rival gang.

The undead oblige, jerking into motion like marionettes.

Aiming pistols and shotguns, his men open fire. Most ape their boss, spraying and snatching at shots, though a curly-haired ginger youth armed with a chunky revolver takes more care.

Floyd shakes his head. *Amateurs.*

One zombie, a middle-aged female with hair pulled into a tight bun, takes lead in the right-hand side of its gut. It spins but lurches on. A big, vest-wearing male freezes, blood fountaining from its dome of a forehead; redhead thug grins. Next to be hit is a sports-gear-clad female no older than fifteen. The slug holes its thigh; it staggers on.

The gang continue their advance. They obviously want to shrink the gap to make their shots count, but they're getting *too* close.

The swiftest zomb – a muscular, topless skinhead covered in tattoos and blood – has reached the garden wall. It trips over the brickwork; as a result, a shot from ginger gangster misses its bald head by a whisker. Up gets the brute. A rattle from Rowbottom's rifle ruins its right arm. Yet still it charges, accelerating. Like a silverback gorilla it pounces on Nidge. Immediately, the hulking beast is torn to shreds by gunfire, with everyone turning their weapons on the 'mong' mauling their brother.

Meaning the other zombies are free to proceed.

Shit. Dis is goin' be bad.

Gibbo must share Floyd's forecast, because he rushes forward to lend assistance. Ironically, the former is more capable than most of his comrades. He blasts two foes in quick succession; the ginger-haired man brings down a third.

Dis could be our chance to escape. While dey distracted.

The other gangsters have stopped shooting skinhead zomb, but they're too slow. Two of them are taken to the pavement, screaming as their vital fluids spray.

Let's go. Leg it quick before it's too late. Floyd's uncharacteristically hesitant, however.

Both Jada and Brad are looking at him now, silently imploring him for approval to flee.

Something's staying his hand. An instinct rankles, and it's not fear, either. He shakes his head and ignores his friends' impatient disbelief.

Then Rowbottom goes down. None of the other mobsters notice as a teenaged zombie claws at their leader.

Kill him! Backing the undead feels bizarre, but it's the survivors' best chance of redemption.

A shot rings out, louder and sharper yet further away than the rest. The shellsuit-clad fiend on top of Rowbottom sags, its head cratered.

Now Floyd remembers: the gang have another member, who's back at their base. Nidge mentioned that the fellow had a sniper rifle; apparently, he knows how to use it. *If we'd tried to run, dat sniper would've shot us instead.*

Covered in blood and brains, Rowbottom gets to his feet. He walks over the playpen and slays the baby-zomb. Next he turns his weapon on one of his men: badly-bitten, bleeding on the ground, redheaded thug is executed without a moment's hesitation. *Pretty sensible, I guess. He could've turned into one o' dem.* Nevertheless, the dark-eyed man's sang-froid is disconcerting.

The battle is won. Three gangsters are dead. A couple of the victors, twin brothers, are disconsolate, but if the loss bothers their leader, he doesn't let on.

In fact, as they walk the final hundred yards to Roosevelt Heights, the self-styled 'Pimp Daddy', striding at the front, becomes more verbose. He regales his followers with his vision for the future. "The world's never gonna recover from this, ya know. These fuckers're gonna spread everywhere. It's gonna be like Mad Max, wi' zombies. Men like me'll be the new kings 'n' presidents when the dust settles." He looks over his shoulder at his shell-shocked crew. "'N' you boys, you'll be my dukes. No, *warlords*. We're gonna build an empire, boys."

His new second-in-command, a mixed race twenty-something known as Sanky, quickens his pace to catch up with his supremo. "Like ya said, Danny. Money'll be worth nothin'. But we stockin' up on the new currency." He leers at Jada, who looks at the ground. "Nice piece of arse, that one. You tapped that, Danny, innit?"

Brad bridles, appears ready to retort.

"Fer a bit. Never mind that now. We're 'ome."

Twenty storeys of sober, grey concrete, Roosevelt Heights actually looks like a penitentiary. From a third floor window, the sharpshooter that saved Rowbottom offers the group a jaunty salute. They're in the car park at the foot of the building, stood in the shade of another high-rise. Private Nelson welcomes respite from the sun's blaze but is anxious about his fate. He needs to keep his cool. *Be ready to take advantage if dese scumbags fuck up.*

The chief eyeballs the three prisoners, hands on hips. "Right. We'll take 'er upstairs. Same floor as the other birds. Gibbo, stay down 'ere wi' these two wankers. They give ya any grief, shoot 'em." Rowbottom catches Floyd's eye. "Keep an eye on this one. Soldier-boy. Shifty-lookin' cunt, he is. The nerdy one looks pretty useless." He turns his back on his male prisoners. "Be back down when I've settled my little Jadie in."

The side door opens, and in go most of the gang and their newest prize.

Gibbo sits on a car bonnet and, patting his knee with his pistol butt, watches his charges like a hawk. "He's gonna kill ya, innit. Sorry boys."

Neither Brad nor Floyd respond.

"Ya might as well sit down." The thug indicates a bench by a rusting playground. "Be comfortable in yer last moments." He smirks, then points his gun. "It wasn't a suggestion. Sit the fuck down, knobheads."

Obeying, Floyd senses Brad's gaze on the side of his face. *He expects me to come up with somefin'. But what? I's not a fuckin' genius, Brad. Stop starin' at me 'n' let me fink.*

Breathing more slowly, the AWOL serviceman tries to empty his mind. *Need to chill out. Fink rationally.*

A scream in the block of flats spoils his meditative efforts. *'Ope dat wasn't Jada. Poor gal. She gonna be used like a piece o' meat. 'N' me 'n' Brad, we're gonna be shot out 'ere. We'll die for nuttin', 'n' no one'll know why.*

He shakes his head. *A pointless death, jus' like Gurdeep. What a fuckin' shit-show.*

Chapter 71 — Jada Blakowska — 15:40

The apartment is dark. She's the only one in this room, but there are other women here, nearby. One of them screamed a minute ago; then she was hit and yelled at, and she didn't make another sound.

What if they killed her? What if they kill me *next?*

"Calm down, idiot," she whispers. "Panickin' will get you nowhere."

Jada can't see anything, so she focusses on other sensory inputs. Voices rumble through the wall; someone guffaws with laughter; somebody else weeps; outside, guns fire, and an aeroplane rumbles overhead. Two smells are prominent, the strongest cannabis, with mildew an undertone. Also, somewhere out in the corridor perhaps, there's a reek that's becoming all too familiar, that of decaying bodies. Her sense of touch is almost useless, for her hands are now bound to a bed leg, but she feels cold handcuffs, the edge of a blanket on a rough mattress. Only one taste is in her mouth: blood, from Danny's friend's slap before he bundled her into the cell.

That bastard Rowbottom. What did I ever see in him, apart from the swagger, chiselled features an' toned physique? In truth, she knew he was a bad match, but like many of her friends, younger Jada made poor relationship choices. Soon enough, his cruel streak trumped the chemistry between them. Will their brief liaison mean he treats her worse or better than the other sex slaves he's collected?

I don't plan to find out. 'Cause I've got through worse than this over the last few days. They didn't search my backpack, so the meds should still be in there. As soon as a chance presents —

A key turns in the lock, sending chills down her spine. The door opens. Jada blinks at the slice of light. Then she recoils as a figure blocks some of the illumination, though she can't move far due to her cuffs. The chains jingle; the shadow in the doorway chuckles.

She gulps. "Danny?"

"The one 'n' only. Comfortable?"

"Fuck you."

Again he laughs. "You've got fire in ya, Jadie. I liked that about ya. There was a lot I liked about ya."

"You got a funny way o' showin' it."

"You're *special*, Jadie. That's why I've not let the lads 'ave a go on ya, like the other birds."

"Lucky me."

"Yeah. Lucky you. 'N' lucky me too. Couldn't believe it when I saw ya, at the Quays. Like ya were sent by God."

She should be scared, picking her words with care, but she's too angry. "What are you talkin' about?"

Still he doesn't move from the threshold; still he looms, a menace absorbing the light. "Did ya not 'ear me outside? When I was talkin' 'bout the future?"

"Your delusions of grandeur?"

"Not delusions, Jadie."

"Even if they're not, what's that gotta do with me?"

"Like I said, you're special. To me. Ya know you're the only bird who's ever dumped me? All the others, I was the one cuttin' loose. But you were different."

"I got standards. That's all. Didn't wanna be messed 'round by a player anymore."

"I wasn't playin' ya, Jadie."

"That's how it seemed. Anyway, I don't wanna argue about somethin' from years ago. That's all in the past —"

"— Not for me." Suddenly, Rowbottom's in the room, by her side, cupping her chin in his hands. There's alcohol on his breath; a musky scent envelops her.

Jada's breath catches in her throat. "Just let me go, Danny. I won't tell anyone where you are. I won't grass you up —"

"— Grass me up fer what? I'm doin' nothin' wrong. Jus' adaptin' t' the times."

"Danny. Surely you see this is wrong. What you're doin, kidnappin' girls, usin' 'em. I mean, ya were dodgy when we were together, but this, an' the shit you've been doin' over the last coupla years… it's on a different level. Ya can stop, though. Ya can let me go, let the others go, walk away —"

"— No. Sorry, darlin', but that ain't 'appenin'. Fair dues, I know this whole operation's a bit on top. 'N' yer right, I 'ave changed. But ya know why?"

Keep him talkin'. "Why?"

"'Cause o' you, Jadie." His voice thickens. "Ya broke my 'eart. I ain't never been the same since then —"

"— Come on, Danny. We were only an item for five minutes."

"Five *months*. 'N' three days. T' be exact. You 'urt me, 'n' all the girls I've pimped out since then, they've all been 'urt 'cause o' *you*. This that's 'appenin' t' ya, 'n' the other birds, is *your* fault."

"That's fuckin' ridiculous, Danny."

"Ya think so? Well, ya know what the most ridiculous part is?"

"What?"

His face is ninety percent shadowed, but she can see a grin forming. "Yer not even gonna be punished fer it. Fer breakin' m' heart. The birds I've pimped, 'n' the new lot, the slaves, *they'll* be punished instead —"

"— They don't have to be," Jada insists. "You can let 'em go. Let me go —"

"— They *do* 'ave t' be punished. Not fer the sake of it, like. They'll be the *cornerstone* of m' new empire, see. But *you*, you'll be rewarded, not punished."

"What?"

"Yeah, fucked up, innit? That's what Nidge said, but he's dead now anyway. *You're* gonna be my queen, Jadie. Once ya can be trusted, I'll take off these cuffs, 'n' you'll be the queen of my new… what d'ya call it? *Regime*, that's it."

"Queen? What the fuck, Danny?"

"Yeah. There's gonna be a lotta changes in this country, includin' the likes o' me gettin' real power fer a change. Ya can blame them fuckin' zombie mongs fer that."

The gangster continues to ramble, but Jada's barely listening. *He's an absolute lunatic. I'm stuck with a lunatic, while Lena's dyin'. Brad an' Floyd probably haven't got long left. An' fuck knows what's goin' on with Luke 'n' Connor 'n' Evie. I need to get outta this mess, somehow.*

A gunshot outside is followed by a second. Of course, hearing weaponry is nothing new, but these shots are closer. Within yards, in fact. *Shit. Were those for Brad an' Floyd? Have they been killed so soon?*

Danny Rowbottom was midway through describing their potential offspring; now he's silent. The turning of cogs in his mind is almost audible. "Weird. I told 'em t' keep yer mates alive fer now." He stands but doesn't leave.

Torn between wanting his malevolent presence gone and fearing what he might report on his return, Jada feels nauseous. A tear trickles down her cheek. *Please leave me alone. But please don't let them be dead.* She clears her throat and prepares to adopt a different tone. Bitterness and disdain won't get her what she wants. "Do my friends really have to die, Danny?" she asks as sweetly as she can stomach. "I mean, Brad has rich parents. Ya could ransom him. An' Floyd's a soldier, so he could be useful."

221

"Leave the thinkin' t' me, darlin'. I'll be back soon."

The door clicks shut behind him, plunging her into darkness once more. It's warm and airless in the flat, yet Jada feels a chill she can't shake. *What's goin' on with Brad an' Floyd?* Her ears strain; she hears nothing of note. The girl in one of the nearby flats is sobbing again, or perhaps it's one of the others. *How many has Rowbottom managed to get in the last forty-eight hours? Has he already killed some?* Of course, her deranged gaoler said Jada is special, his 'queen', so she should be safe for the time being. *Unless he loses his temper. He's always had a short fuse.*

However, this is not the time for aimless speculation. If Brad and Floyd have indeed been killed, Jada is responsible for her own salvation. Once more, she rattles her cuffs. They're firmly held in place.

Footsteps in the corridor outside. *Is he back already?* The tread rumbles past her door. *No, not him. But I need to be quiet.* Her fingers trace her handcuffs' chain to the bed post. *Maybe I can raise the bed by lyin' underneath an' pushin' upwards with my legs, like the leg press at the gym.* Down the metal support, to the cheap carpet, where a round base plate, its circumference similar to that of a hairspray bottle, is screwed into the floor. *Dammit. Maybe the apartment was leased on a 'furnished' basis, or it was a halfway house for drug addicts… Christ, Jada, it doesn't matter. Focus.*

She needs to unsecure the leg from the floorboards. Gripping the screw heads with her fingers, she tries to twist the fixing loose but only succeeds in chipping a nail. *Ouch.*

Her fingertip tells her the screw is of the flat blade variety. *A tool. I need a tool.* Stretching her legs, she prods around under the bed. Her foot catches on an item of clothing, but nothing of any use. *Yer gettin' desperate. Face it. Ya just need to wait for Danny to come back, hope he doesn't change his mind an' decide to kill ya, then watch for a better opportunity to escape.*

In the meantime, though, Lena's dying. Telling the CEO's story has become an obsession for Jada, one which will prompt her to take dangerous risks, but also one she's not yet willing to forsake. Plus, those gunshots may not have been fired at her friends. So, if she escapes, she might be able to save them. By biding her time, she could be sentencing Adderley, Private Nelson and Brad Li to death.

Gotta get these cuffs off, now. I need *to get out of here.*

She still needs a tool, however, and all the desperation in the world won't force one to materialise. Her backpack is empty, save from the supplies for treating Lena. Jada checks her pockets: nothing. *Surely there's something, on my person, I can use…*

Her jeans zipper. She tests its edge; it feels roughly suitable for the task at hand. Now she only has to pull it free of the zip.

Two minutes later, she hasn't made any progress. Nevertheless, she continues to wrench and tear, breaking two fingernails.

Someone is in the corridor, their footfalls heavy and ponderous. Jada holds her breath. Sweat prickles her hairline. Her pulse spikes.

The steps pass by her door; she exhales. In her anxiety, she's removed the zipper. *Yes!* The tiny article isn't a perfect fit for the bed screws. But with a lot of jimmying, and even more cursing, she uproots the leg. Then she lies on her back. She can't position her whole backside under the bed due to the location of her arms, so she has to settle for a single leg push.

Gritting her teeth, she strains at the steel frame. It budges a millimetre; she needs about an inch to slip the handcuff chain clear. *Jeez, why is this thing so heavy? It's not that long since I last went to the gym.*

For the fourth time, someone's heading towards her prison. Their approach is quieter, softer. She recalls Danny's visit earlier, when she didn't realise he was there until his key was in the lock. *It's him.* Again she heaves, to no avail. *He's comin', an' he'll be breathin' all over me, gettin' too close.*

A third attempt: this time she finds a strength she never knew she possessed. Up goes the bed. She drags the cuffs from under the bed post and scrambles to her feet just as the key clicks. The handle turns.

With a growl of terror-charged fury, Jada rushes the door. As it opens she leaps. Lands on Rowbottom, her still-bound hands high. He's taken by surprise and knocked to the ground; her knees on his torso drive the wind from his lungs. Fingers laced, she pounds at his face with both fists. At first he whimpers and struggles. Then he stops.

Warm liquid is on Jada's wrists and knuckles. Beneath her, in the corridor's wan light, Danny's once-comely face is a mess of bruises and blood. He's unconscious but still wheezing. After a moment of staring at his blood on own skin, she climbs off him. She rifles through his pockets, finds a small key and unfastens her manacles. *Time to go.*

Yet now more footsteps are coming her way. She looks in both directions. The end of the corridor is to her right, the fire escape there blocked by furniture, and to the left there are half a dozen apartment doors, then a corner. Two, maybe three people are nearing the bend.

They'll have guns. An' they're gonna get me back for hurtin' Danny.

Chapter 72 — Floyd Nelson — 15:55

Something's happening in the tower block. There were shouts, two shotgun blasts and a number of thuds. *Must be loud to hear dem all da way down 'ere.*

Importantly for Floyd and Brad, their guard, Gibbo, is nervous. He's already had to shoot two firefighter zombies that emerged from behind De Gaulle Heights. His vigilance earned him a commendation from Rowbottom when the boss came to investigate the gunfire, but the encounter left the thug skittish. He's alternating between glaring at his two detainees, at Roosevelt Heights, and at the fire engine half-obscured by De Gaulle. His lips are working, his eyebrows jewelled with perspiration.

For a third time, Floyd tries to catch Brad's eye. On this occasion, he succeeds, and they share a look that says everything. *We need to make a move. Use da guy's distraction to our advantage. He's ten metres away. Only has to look away for two seconds to give us enough time...* Now he looks at the window, where Rowbottom's sniper was posted earlier. The glass is dark, the curtains drawn.

"What ya gawpin' at each other fer?" Gibbo snarls. "Don't be gettin' any fuckin' ideas, right?"

Another gunshot and a high-pitched shrill. Gibbo takes four steps towards his base, then the same number backwards. Glass smashes somewhere near the other building, jerking his head that way.

Now. We need to do it now.

The soldier switches from drilled-to-attention to battle-stations in a heartbeat. Keeping low, moving more like an animal than a human, he covers the distance between his starting position and his foe's before the gangster can aim his gun. By the Brad his friend reacts, Floyd's already winning. He's stronger, fitter and faster. Soon he has Rowbottom's henchman disarmed and pinned down. A hard punch in the mouth subdues the struggling Mancunian, who stinks of several layers of grime and sweat.

Brad secures victory by scooping up the dropped pistol and pointing it, safety off, at Gibbo's head. "Shall I shoot 'im?" He's out of breath, even though he's barely moved.

"No." Floyd turns Gibbo onto his front, tears off a strip of the man's t-shirt and uses it as a gag. Then he pulls the belt from his prisoner's waist and binds his wrists. Finally, he reclaims the commando knife Gibbo stole from him upon capture. "Pass me da gun," he tells Brad.

Brad obeys. "That was pretty awesome, bro."

"No biggie, fam. Listen up. Our tower's nearby, yeah?"

"'Bout 'alf a mile from 'ere, t' the south. I think."

"Get back dere 'n' tell 'em what's happened. Get some weapons. Maybe bring Luke back with ya. Ya get me?"

"Yeah. What're you gonna do?"

"Go get Jada, obvs."

"I should come. There's shitloads of 'em in there —"

"— Which is why we need backup 'n' weapons. But in da meantime, Jada could be gettin' killed, or hurt, so let's get a move on."

"Course." Brad scampers away, darting from vehicle to tree to vehicle.

Floyd checks the stolen pistol, a Beretta 9000. The same model was used in the murder of one of his schoolmates. *Four 9mm Parabellum rounds. Not enough, but it'll have to do for now.* Staying low, he dashes towards Roosevelt. He doesn't head for the door used by the gang, though. Instead, he finds a ground floor window without bars and uses the pistol to smash the pane then scrape away the jagged shards of glass. After a final glance over his shoulder, Floyd climbs into the building.

The kitchen reeks of old cigarette smoke and dead mice. He pauses to listen. When satisfied he's alone in the residence he advances. Opens the front door. Checks both ways in the corridor. Nothing. Going to the left takes him to the stairs on this side of the block, which he uses, treading as lightly as he's able, to ascend to the fourth storey. *Dat's where dat sniper was before. Dey probably all on da same floor.*

He hopes so, anyway. Because he may not have the time to search the whole building.

At the stairwell exit, he stops again and holds his breath. Someone's shouting, but the words are unintelligible. A door's taking a battering. No gunfire, though. Floyd peers through the porthole window and sees nothing, before shouldering the door wide.

Out on the third floor. Heart's pounding in his skull. Hands squeezing the Beretta so hard it hurts. A female's crying. Timber's crunching. A woman shouts. *Dat Jada?*

Floyd masters the urge to fly down the passageway and round the corner with all guns blazing. *Outnumbered, outgunned. Better trainin', dough, so make use o' dat. Don't give away yer only advantage, Private Nelson.* Therefore, he creeps down the corridor, and when he reaches the turn, he backs into the wall and readies his weapon. Inhales slowly through his nose and exhales orally.

In one fluid movement, he steps out and swivels. Twenty paces away, three men are attempting to break into an apartment. One responds and points a shotgun. Floyd points and fires, going for centre mass now he's not fighting the dead. As the shotgunner drops, a red patch expanding on his white basketball vest, his killer twitches his hands to aim at the second quickest on the draw. Two taps; the sniper, hit in the solar plexus, drops his rifle. Floyd withdraws as four shots are loosed by the survivor. Three of the rounds hit the corner, splintering plaster. A fourth holes the wall opposite Nelson. Someone else is coming, their shoes echoing down the corridor.

Now the sniper's moaning in pain. *I got one shot left, 'n' da knife. Sounds like two enemies 'round da corner now. Three weapons between 'em.* The shotgun barks, as if to confirm.

Thirty seconds pass. No one moves. *Dey know I'm a soldier. Dey scared. Dey don't know I only got one round left.* Even so, Floyd can't win this fight. He simply needs to get his enemies away from that door, in case it's Jada on the other side. They're locked out; the woman must be causing them problems. And if anybody is likely to cause them problems, it's Jada.

What to do now, though? Rushing them will lead to almost-certain death. Waiting could mean Jada gets harmed, or taken hostage and used against him. Floyd's met her only yesterday and doesn't even know her surname, but she's one of his squadmates. Which means he won't leave her behind.

Someone calls out from one of the flats he's passed. The voice is female, frightened, pleading but hopeful, as though emboldened by the conflict in the corridor. *Perhaps dat's Jada? Nah… she sounds foreign. So what, dough? Whateva, it's some gal who needs help. Come on, Floyd. Make a decision, fam.*

A distraction.

That's what's required.

So he'll backtrack, release the trapped lady and, with a little luck, discover some means of beguiling Rowbottom and his crew. *Stab in da dark, bruv. But better odds dan takin' on two guys who know I's comin', with one 9mm round.* As stealthily as his leather boots will allow – partly to keep his opponents guessing but mainly so he can hear the abductee he's seeking – he retraces his steps.

The foreign girl must either have superb hearing or extrasensory perception, because she detects his motion before he's within fifteen feet of number 316, which is ten yards from the stairway. "Hallo! Is somebody there? Help, please!"

The private freezes. "Shh. You in three-one-six? Answer quietly."

"Yes," she hisses. "Please hurry. I not safe."

Yer not da only one, luv. Floyd's bracing himself to boot the door when he hears a curious noise. A scrabbling, almost animal sound is coming from number 318, not from the door itself, but somewhere *inside* the flat. He wrinkles his nostrils. The insidious stench of the undead is becoming more familiar with every passing hour.

He shakes his head. *No time for fuckin' about or second guessin'.* A sharp, economical kick compromises the lock. He's in. At first he ignores the pitiful woman chained to a bed frame. He's listening, in case the sex-traffickers have found the courage to give chase. All is silent, apart from the bound girl's tears and the scratching from next door. When he tries the light, the naked bulb hanging from the ceiling sparks then sputters and pops. A wall-length window in the far wall, presumably for the balcony, has closed blinds, so the living room remains shrouded in gloom.

The captive is Far Eastern, with the tan of a Vietnamese or Cambodian. Her small face is mottled by contusions, her cuffed wrists raw, her leggings and vest torn and stained. Pulling the bed post from the floor barehanded proves fruitless, so Floyd uses his knife to rip the base free of the boards.

"Thank you." She stands, wobbles for a moment and steadies herself on Nelson's arm. "We need go now. Something in there." The petite woman points at the wall dividing 316 from 318. "You hear? It try get in!"

Floyd resheathes his dagger. "What's your name?"

"Mony."

"'Ow many of you are dere?"

"Huh?"

"How many girls?"

"Three. I with one girl, in same room. But now she move room."

One o' dem's turned zombie. Mony's handcuffs are cheap, the sort used for BDSM rather than police issue, so Floyd uses his knife handle to smash them open. "Wait here, okay?"

She sits on the bed as he tiptoes back across the room. Now he can hear chatter from the corridor, deep voices raised in protest. The gangsters are getting braver. Then there's a tapping on the window behind him; Mony gasps and hugs her knees.

Still listening for his enemies, Floyd sneaks over to the balcony door. He fiddles with the blind adjusting spindle. Almost jumps out of his skin when he sees the pale, dead-eyed blonde girl on the other side of the window. For a couple of heartbeats, the undead sex slave doesn't move. Then it lunges forwards, making Nelson recoil when it butts the glass. Its tongue smears saliva and blood on the pane. *Like it's tryin' to kiss me.*

A plan in mind, the squaddie recloses the blinds, catches Mony's eye, raises a finger to his lips, drags a coffee table across the room towards the exit, picks up a vase from the mantelpiece and leaves the apartment. He steels himself. Kicks open the door to room 318. Waits a moment, staring into the darkness, nostrils flaring at the rancid odour within. Hears shuffling, wet noises, fingers squeaking on glass. Then footsteps, slow at first but increasing in tempo. The first he sees of the blonde zombie is its eyes, and that's when he retreats and throws the vase towards the bullet-ridden corridor corner. He slips back into 316 as the ornament smashes. Finally, he closes the broken door too and pushes the coffee table into place.

The furniture shakes and shifts; the crack of light from the corridor widens. Heaving with all his might, the soldier shoves the table to reseal the exit.

Briefly, the monster assaults the door, and Floyd worries his tactics will fail. However, after a handful of blows, the dead girl quits. Her uneven footsteps go to the left, then the right, becoming fainter.

Private Nelson lifts the table in order to move it without unnecessary noise. After removing his boots, he opens the door, grimacing at the hinge's creak. He steps into the corridor, pistol ready. The zombie's plodding towards the corner. *Hurry up, gal.*

Tentative footfalls are coming from the gangsters' position. Men whisper to each other.

Moving silently thanks to his unshod feet, Floyd follows the fair-haired monster. He prays it doesn't turn. *Do dey smell us? Sniff out our brains 'n' blood, 'n' shit?*

Shattered vase crunches under the zombie's ballet shoes.

The hushed voices become more frantic.

Zomb-girl reaches the corner. It pauses, still obscured by the wall, as if for dramatic effect, giving Floyd the opportunity to catch up. He's only six metres behind the foul-smelling, boob-tube and jeans-wearing beast.

It steps into the open.

Rowbottom's boys blurt out obscenities.

Nelson darts forwards as shots are fired. He catches the bulletholed corpse before it can topple backwards. Moving at a half-crouch, he propels the body before himself, using it as an inhuman shield. More slugs and buckshot hit the zombie. Floyd glimpses two men over its shoulder; they're no more than ten feet away. He gives the bloodied carcass a final push, then fires his Beretta. Draws his knife and throws it.

One of the gangster twins vomits blood onto the dagger hilt protruding from his throat. His brother is on his knees, wheezing, his bare chest punctured an inch above the sternum. Already, the youth's eyes are glassy.

Shivering, Floyd pulls his knife out of the choking twin's neck, giving the blade a twist to end the suffering. He checks the zombie to make sure it's dead, collects the fallen guns, steps over the two men he slew earlier and knocks on the damaged door halfway down the corridor. "Jada?"

"Floyd?" She sounds distant, traumatised. "I'm in here." Once she's cleared the blockage at her door, she falls into Floyd's arms, quivering.

"Where's da boss, Rowbottom?"

"He's dead. I strangled him with my handcuffs." She presents her still-bound hands; fresh tears spill from reddened eyes. "I killed him, Floyd. I killed him. I killed him. Floyd... I —"

"— I know. It's alright. There are still one or two o' dem left, somewhere, so let's get outta 'ere."

The East Asian girl is nowhere to be found. They don't have time to save everyone they encounter, though, so Floyd and Jada leave Roosevelt Heights.

"Where's Brad?" she asks. Blinking in the sunlight, she holds her nose.

"Sent him for backup." Hands on hips, he takes a moment. *My days, sumfin' stinks real bad.* "He went dat way." He points in the direction of De Gaulle Heights. "In fact," he squints, "is dat him?"

It is him. Running, no, *sprinting*, he's not alone. It appears that, somehow, Brad's managed to attract every zombie in Salton. And he's heading their way, waving and shouting.

Chapter 73 — Randall Maguire — 16:10

The Irishman flexes his trigger finger. Of course, he fired plenty of rounds in training, but he doesn't remember his hands hurting afterwards. *Yer gettin' old, laddie.* He's used most of his ammunition. For all of his shooting, he only hit three of the troops in black. Bloody Jones was responsible for many more, firing with such precision and cunning that they beat back a foe with an overwhelming numerical advantage. The drone scrambled by HQ – prompted no doubt by a growing concern among the higher-ups about the mysterious paramilitaries – secured the triumph, though it didn't arrive until ten minutes ago.

By then, Maguire and his aide were exhausted and shaken. The latter was winded, too, thanks to a slug stopped by his flak jacket. The former was relatively unscathed, save for splinters, scratches and grazes earned by using tree trunks, tree roots and thorny shrubs for cover as they defended their position on the bank of the canal.

"Come on, then, sir," Jones urges. "I think we've established the way's clear."

There's no mockery in the fighter's tone, but his boss accepts the criticism anyway. The enemy are beaten for now; he needs to press on and make up for lost time. So he nods, puffs his cheeks and follows his henchman down the treacherous woodland path.

He should be full of verve and optimism, as his luck's begun to change. When he made a desperate call to base at three PM, he expected to receive short shrift at best, and reprisals against his family at worst. Instead, the request proved profitable. As well as resulting in the deployment of a rescue drone to help overcome the MIBs, he's received intel. This morning, another UAV spotted a man matching Private Nelson's description entering one of the flats less than a kilometre away. The deserter's fingerprints in the boat merely indicated that he'd disembarked at this stage of the canal, but actual footage of the serviceman was proof positive. Plus, they now have a physical location on which to focus: Churchill Heights.

He *should* be full of verve and optimism, but he's not. Being under heavy fire was demoralising. In order to secure the safety of his wife and son, he'll probably have to endure worse. And although his superiors have been forgiving, even supportive thus far, their charity will end the minute Maguire fails. Or even if he succeeds. *Might see me as a loose end...*

Trudging through mud, he makes himself a promise. *Soon as this is done, we're on a plane to somewhere untraceable. Me, Caylie, an' Ronan. Outta their clutches forever.*

When will it be 'done', though? When Maguire's fixed the Adderley situation, he will probably be expected to turn his attention to dealing with the outbreak itself. Erasing any trace of official culpability is but the first stage of a process that could drag on for months. One which may require the total annihilation of Greater Manchester, perhaps the whole of the northwest of England. *Yer gettin' ahead o' yerself, man. Deal wi' Nelson an' Adderley first. Then reassess.*

The miasma of decaying bodies in the canal fades, replaced for a few moments by that of vegetation and soil. The breather is short-lived, however. They pass a house in a clearing. Surrounded by zombie corpses, it appears to have been hit by an explosion.

As the two government employees emerge from the trees, the high-rise flats in sight, the agent receives a message, with an .mp4 file attached, from the office. CCTV images, captured this morning by a camera fitted to Chamberlain Heights, depict an injured female being carried into Churchill shortly before Nelson's arrival. The resolution is grainy. A brief shot of the woman's face, frozen and magnified, is not conclusive. Nevertheless, it strengthens Maguire's conviction. *It's her. It's Lena Adderley. The private an' his new buddies took her into that tower. Maybe to rest up for a bit, while she recovers from whatever injuries she's taken.*

He shows Jones the video. Then Adderley's photograph.

The Welshman folds his arms and makes a face. When pushed, he admits the wounded woman resembles the Evolve CEO, but he's not as convinced as Maguire. *He doesn't have to be. I know it was her. I know it was Nelson seen by the drone. An' I call the shots. It's my job, reputation, family on the line.*

Consequently, the agent's next decision is made without hesitation. His application for assault troops is accepted, with an ETA of twenty minutes. In the meantime, a missile strike will be followed by a heavy drone bombardment. None of the measures are authorised lightly. He has to argue his case with vigour. When he ends the call, satisfied, he's as drained as he was after the gunfight by the canal.

"Now all we have to do is wait," he tells Jones.

"Somewhere a little more... sheltered, maybe?" the younger man suggests.

They take cover behind a burnt-out estate car.

"Looks like someone's already had a go, see." Jones points at the building facing Churchill Heights; its other side is blackened and ruined.

Lips pursed, Maguire uses his smartphone to peruse UAV Control's event log. "Yeah. A drone was destroyed here, half-nine this mornin'."

"Standard response is 'nuke the area'?"

"Seems so."

"Jeez. Looks like they use some serious ordnance, it does. So ya soften 'em up with a strike, then throw the drones at 'em, an' we go in after an' try to identify the bits an' pieces?"

"That's the plan. Any minute now —"

The missile streaks down out of the heavens at a dizzying speed. It hits the tower block like a god's hammer to a planet-sized anvil, shaking the ground, the very air, and crumpling walls and windows with ease. Orange fires rage. Black smoke streams. Grey dust billows. Brown dirt showers. A portal to hell has opened, its epicentre the tenth floor of Churchill Heights, Salton, Greater Manchester.

When Maguire tastes grit, he realises he's gaping at the destruction. The smell is overpowering. It feels like the temperature, already over 25°C, has risen a couple of degrees. Although the roar of flames is loud, it seems muted after the sheer violence of the initial detonation. Three comparatively minuscule blasts follow; they're probably caused by boilers overheating and exploding, according to Jones.

Then come the drones. After hours of begging for just one, Maguire's been blessed with four of the squat, ominous machines. Each claiming one side of the square building, they begin at the top. They descend in synchrony, battering concrete and glass with cannonades so chastening that he pities those under fire. *Better them than my family, though. Every day o' the week.* After one sweep, the drones withdraw to hover above the devastated high-rise.

They're ready to swoop in an' deal more death, at my command. The thought makes him feel peculiar, as though he's literally drunk on power.

Simultaneously enraptured and horrified by the ruin he's wrought, Agent Maguire loses track of time. He wonders if there were any living survivors in the Heights, other than Nelson and Adderley. Perhaps he's torn families asunder. Maimed adults and left their children unguarded. Maybe he's slain babies, infants, teens, cursing their parents with the same fate he's so desperate to avoid himself. *What right did I have to do that? What right does* anyone *have, regardless of their motive?*

The whole area has been evacuated, though. Anybody lingering in the flats must know they do so at their own risk. They've had plenty of warnings. They were given every opportunity to follow the rules, leave their homes and go somewhere safe. As ever, the Government has done its utmost to safeguard its citizens, from a danger no one could've foreseen.

Christ, Randall, yer pathetic. A company man, through-and-through, a spineless noddin' dog. Your bosses are partly responsible for this, an' their priority is not to save lives. It's to bury the bad news an' protect 'emselves.

The bark and whipcrack of Jones's rifle jolts Maguire from his reverie. "Sir." The Welshman is no stranger to war zones; he's focussed instead on their surroundings, on potential threats. Sixty metres away, closer to the two towers, a zombie staggers then stumbles to the ground. Again the gun booms. Another figure falls, roughly twenty paces from the first. The soldier lowers his weapon and screws up his face. "You gettin' that? Not the fire, that rotten smell."

"Yeah." The agent spits. "Gettin' worse."

"Probably not good news. Anyway, I reckon it's almost time, it is."

Maguire checks the countdown on his phone. He's received a message, however: the detachment of soldiers, plucked from a battle with zombies near Salton Shopping Centre, has been delayed by a horde of undead to the north.

No matter. At some point in the next hour, Nelson and Adderley will be found and neutralised, and Caylie and Ronan will be safe.

For now.

Chapter 74 — Naomi Adderley — 16:45

Zombies ahead.

She's not scared, though; in fact, the younger Adderley sibling relishes the prospect. While facing the odious abominations on Wendover Avenue made icy slush of her blood, blasting them to hell warmed her heart. It's not a normal reaction, she knows. But these aren't normal times.

Her anticipation rises the faster she rides down the Salton backstreet. Thirty paces short of the handful of dead cannibals, she applies the brakes. The rabble of monsters, ragged-clothed, covered in muck and scarlet stains, lurches towards her when she stops. They reach out to her. Craving sustenance.

Not from me, you ugly bastards. Naomi draws her pistol and, with the faintest of grins, aims for heads. Eight times she pulls the trigger, the vibration in her hands almost orgasmic. Six zombies go down for good, daubing the potholed tarmac in glorious crimson.

I'm coming for you, sis. None of these useless lumps can stop me.

Now she knows where to go, as well. McCall's advice took her in the right direction, but Panucci's call, five minutes ago, has inserted a pin into the map. Not far from the Quays, there's an array of deprived tower blocks. For so long a stain on the Salton skyline, the high-rises are now a beacon of hope. Her Italian friend reported a missile and drone strike on one of the buildings – Naomi heard the former for herself. More crucially, he has somehow hacked MoD communications, revealing an ongoing priority search for Lena Adderley, with a building named Churchill Heights the presumed location. Pepe will incur the harshest of penalties if caught, so he's owed an enormous debt.

Stopping at a crossroads to get her bearings, Naomi sniffs the air. The reeks of fire and dust, both present everywhere in the county, are stronger than ever. Yet there's something else. Something even more noticeable. Cloying her nostrils. Clinging to her tonsils. It's the sickly bouquet of meat in decay. Worse than it was in the service station. Which doesn't make sense, for that was in a confined space. In order for the stench to be as tangible in the open, there must be dozens, or hundreds of the zombies within fifty yards. But she sees none; she hears nothing.

Naomi continues to ride, cutting through a depressing council estate. She reaches a hill's summit and stops. Using her hand as a visor, she espies the glass structures of Salton Quays glinting in the sun. In the foreground protrude the solid trunks of the tower blocks, a black plume of smoke spewing from the one closest to the woods. A dual carriageway will take her directly into the midst of the tired monoliths. It may not be the shrewdest option, however. The individuals who coordinated the missile and drone attacks are probably still in the area, and they'll notice her ingress if she roars onto the scene on her throaty Honda.

No point coming all this way just to be shot or arrested.

With that in mind, she crosses the dual carriageway and enters another estate. Undead onlookers tempt her to slow down and test her accuracy, but she's already decided that, if they're not in her way, she'll exercise restraint. *Pretty sure I can get to the woods this way. Then follow the trees?* There's no time for self-doubt. Her orienteering skills never deserted her while hunting game in the States, so she needs to trust her instincts. Most importantly: keep moving. A massive explosion from the direction of the flats spurs her on. Now she smells burning flesh rather than rotting bodies.

Pushing the bike to its limits, she screeches around corners, dodges overturned wheelie bins and corpses, steers around speed bumps. Soon she reaches a footpath, which, as hoped, leads to the forest. The towers are getting bigger. Riding the dirt track that skirts the treeline makes them larger still. At a distance of approximately two hundred metres, she rolls to a standstill. Four drones, floating and mute like metallic jellyfish, are gathered around the closest of the high-rises.

The yellowing concrete cuboid itself is in a sorry state. *Must've been a helluva missile. If Lena is in there, she'll be lucky to be alive.*

If she isn't, then I'm fresh out of ideas.

Not that she's otherwise full of inspiration. Dismounting, she shakes her head, clicks her tongue. *What now?* She can't simply run across the wasteland, enter the skyscraper and extract her sister. The UAVs will register her approach within seconds, and, judging by the craters pitting the tower's walls, a single burst from one of the robotic sentinels will reduce her to pink mist.

Think, Naomi! Use your brains for something useful for a change.

There's an ashen estate car abandoned in the wasteland. She could dash over, only fifty yards, use the wreck to take shelter, move onto that tree…

Shit!

She hears the armoured personnel carrier long before she sees it. After shoving over the motorcycle, she prostrates herself and prays she won't be sighted.

The bulky vehicle is surprisingly rapid. A trail of dust hangs in its wake as it hurtles between the pair of high-rises and towards the fire-ruined station wagon. As the APC grinds to a halt, two men appear from beside the car. *Good job I didn't use it as cover.* A soldier jumps out of the transport and salutes one of the previously-hidden individuals, who both wear long-sleeved tops and combat trousers and are carrying weapons.

Again, Naomi hears an engine and the roll of heavy wheels, but the APC isn't moving. A second, identical vehicle appears and takes the same path as its predecessor. Another khaki-uniformed man decamps. He too greets the shorter of the two waiting fellows.

And now come the grunts, eight from each truck. They're well-armed, but they look tired.

Four weaponised UAVs. Ten British Army professionals. Two other men with guns. Plus the capability to call airstrikes. *I've got no chance. Big difference between shooting bumbling zombies with a bike to scoot me away if they get too close, and taking on trained men with assault rifles and advanced tech.*

But her sister is in that tower, which means surrender is out of the question. She'll be in Lena's corner no matter the odds. She always has been and always will be. As their father taught: one doesn't give up on family. Brute force won't work, though, so she'll rely on her intellect instead.

Naomi's eyes flicker between the troops, who continue to converse with the plain-clothes operatives, and the smoking hulk of Churchill Heights, picketed by airborne death-bots. *Lena, and whoever is with her, must know they're being watched. If they're still alive. They'll see the drones. They've probably spotted the soldiers, too, with the noise those APCs made. And they'll be terrified of another missile.* "They'll be desperate to get out," she mutters. "But they'll need a distraction."

Momentarily, she laments the selection of firearms chosen by Panucci. The handgun and shotgun are prefect for tackling the undead, but a rifle of some sort, a long range tool, would be better at this juncture. *No matter. I'll work with what I've got.*

She barely thinks about the next few steps. After wrestling the Honda upright, mounting and turning the ignition key, Naomi aims her pistol in the general direction of the troops. Three times she fires. Then she rides, gunning the engine, kicking up dust on the dirt track. A quick glance to the left shows soldiers taking cover. One of the drones is on the move; bile rises in her throat.

When she reaches the corner of the wasteland, where it meets the treeline, she follows the track north. Now she's at least one hundred yards from the Army detachment. The drone, meanwhile, is bearing her way. She aims another three rounds in the direction of the APCs and rides on, heading north.

After fifty yards Naomi fires at the UAV, which is scanning the woods. *Please send another. Please send another.* Her prayers are heard, for a second drone is mobile.

The squaddies are on the move, heading to intercept Naomi as she rounds the wasteland. A rifle crackles: down go two of the men. Four of them stop to return fire at Churchill Heights. The remainder drop to the ground and shoot at the bike-riding woman. While most of the lead misses by a distance, two rounds pass within inches.

She's reaching the north-eastern corner of the field when a second volley from the tower drops another pair of troops. The soldiers have slowed down, with more targetting the smoking high-rise. Except that they're now firing lower. *Why? Are Lena and her friends on the ground?* Naomi can't see and doesn't have time to get a better look. Because in another two hundred yards, she'll pass the other building, Chamberlain Heights, and she can turn right. Make her own getaway.

Two of them out of the way should give Lena enough of a chance. I'll have done more than enough, won't I?

However, the problem hasn't been solved; it's been shared. Naomi will soon be well within range for the two UAVs yet to move. The roaming drones aren't far away, either, though they're moving slower than she expected. A flurry of automatic gunfire, causing her to duck, reminds her of the threat from the infantry. She's made life easier for her sister, yet much harder for herself.

Fifty yards to Chamberlain Heights. The twin drones are motionless, emotionless, poised to reduce her and the motorbike to a jumble of scrap metal, bones and masticated flesh. A glance to her left: the soldiers aren't aiming at her anymore. They're firing instead between the two towers. *Lena's getting away!* One of the squaddies collapses with a cry. *Whoever's with her's a helluva shot.*

However, the pair of UAVs Naomi lured out of formation are going to intercept her before she reaches the road. Their cannons rumble. Dust erupts from the ground split-seconds before she passes. She coughs. Squints. Cringes. Pulls the handlebars right in desperation. Twenty paces short of the first block of flats, so she rides over a dip. The wheels leave the ground; her stomach somersaults. Tyres squeal as she lands in a yard. Immediately she has to swerve past a recycling bin. Then a yellow skip. She's losing control. But there's a fence ahead, its gate open.

If I can just get through there, turn left, I'll be on the other side of Chamberlain, and I can turn right onto the access road, speed out of here — Bang-bang-bang behind Naomi. One of the drones. It unloads again, raining hellfire. *Through the gate. I just need to get through the gate!*

Something explodes under her backside. *Tyre's gone.* And she's flying, almost in slow motion, back down again… then thud, then blackout.

Chapter 75 — Luke Norman — 18:00

They're not going to make it. By drawing the attention of the half of the drones, plus the soldiers, the mystery motorcyclist has given them a chance. But their window of opportunity is narrow, the margin for error too slim. Transporting the deadweight of Lena is a Herculean task; herding the kids, under-fire, is impossible. The air around them buzzes with bullets. Above them hunter/killers zip around, their cannon thundering in the sunshine. Although their transport, the bus Gould observed, is only around the corner, the couple of hundred yard dash feels like ten miles.

Too tired fer this shit. Legs like lumps of iron.

The atmosphere has changed. No longer composed of nitrogen and oxygen, it's a sludge. The survivors are wading, not running. And Luke's son is falling behind; in fact, he's stopped altogether.

"Ccoooonnooooorrrrrr!" the father yells. He draws in breath for at least a minute, then calls again.

The youngster's not listening, however. He's turning. Zombies are coming, blackened and singed, missing arms, legs, even chunks of skull, some still aflame from the air strike that extirpated them after they chased Jada, Brad and Floyd from Roosevelt Heights to Churchill.

"Nooooo, Connoooooorrr!" *Why's m' voice like that? As though I'm underwater, or in a slow-mo section o' some shitty movie.*

Luke swivels to go back for his child, who remains standing. Except that, suddenly, Connor's in an elevated position, at the top of a steep, grassy slope. His father tries to run, but wind from the peak beats him down. So he crawls. Clumps of turf tear from the soil as he hauls himself up the hill, which is steepening with every foot he travels.

The kid, meanwhile, is a statue. His arms and legs are motionless, yet somehow he's shrinking, getting more distant. *What the fuck?*

Screaming Connor's name all the while, Luke claws his way up the incline. At least the zombies have left, as have all of his friends. The tower blocks are gone, the drones, soldiers, armoured cars and bus all vanished. There is nothing but the man, the boy and the hill.

Eventually, exhausted, Luke gains the summit. He puts his hands on his son's small shoulders and spins him around one hundred and eighty degrees, only to see the back of his head. Frowning, he repeats the motion and achieves the same result. Again and again he twists his child; over and over he is frustrated. Then, on the tenth attempt, he freezes. All strength leaves his arms, and his stomach roils. *No. Please, God, no.*

Pale-faced and dead-eyed, zombie Connor stares at his dad. Bloodstained teeth are revealed as his mouth opens, gapes, yawns. It widens until the black hole is all Luke can see, till it swallows his head, neck, body...

He sits up straight with a gasp. The hum of the vehicle's electric engine is like something from a science fiction movie, and for a moment, Luke wonders if entry to Connor's mouth has transported him to another dimension. Yet everyone else is with him: Josh Gould, in the driver's cabin; Theo and Gabriela on the bench behind, the latter's head resting on the former's shoulder; Connor and Evie chatting; Floyd and Brad to their rear; Jada next to Ashara; and on the back seat, lay down, hooked up to a rudimentary intravenous drip attached to a seat post, Lena Adderley.

Have we just got outta Mortborough?

No, that was the early hours of yesterday morning. Today is Wednesday, the time early evening.

A missile hit Churchill Heights, choking them with dust and almost crushing them with debris. Drone fire kept their heads down for a while. Private Nelson, Brad Li and Jada Blakowska escaped Rowbottom's gang and were chased by a mass of undead. The second air strike destroyed the horde. Jada produced medication, with which Ashara injected Lena. APCs carrying British Army troops arrived, and it seemed all was lost. However, an anonymous motorcyclist appeared and began to perform laps of the wasteland. The distraction, plus some sharpshooting by Floyd, bought the group enough time to break out of Churchill Heights's northerly exit. Carrying Lena on a stretcher fashioned from a trestle table, they fled. Into the bus Gould espied that afternoon. Away from the flats. A blurry, chastening chase, the hunter/killers overhead, cannon chattering death... But only for a couple of minutes. Because, just as they were about to emerge from the tunnel where the A9015 underpasses Pennington Roundabout, there was an explosion overhead.

Back in the open, they saw a trio of men-in-black above, by the railings overlooking the A-road. One, holding a rocket launcher of some sort, was adjusting his aim. Another of the drones blew up. The two UAVs lagging behind opened fire; the MIBs ran; the slowest was shredded by cannon rounds. Then the bus reached a dip in the road, meaning Luke lost sight of the action.

Gould thought they should find somewhere to hide while they had the chance, so they rolled into Salton Bus Depot. Food was stolen from a nearby convenience shop. A handful of zombies attacked and were repulsed. After eating a sandwich and chatting briefly with Jada, the group held a discussion. Their next port of call was decided democratically. The refugee camp in Manchester was selected over Luke's father's place, with Gould's preference – a journey to London, to the heart of Government – receiving one solitary vote, from the transport supervisor himself. Surprisingly, Josh accepted the result with good grace.

Luke was more disgruntled. Whenever he, Connor and their crew are out of immediate danger, he begins to fear for those not present, and his family's well-being becomes more prominent in his thoughts. But, too weary to argue, he closed his eyes. Sleep overwhelmed him. "How long 'ave I been out?" he asks, stretching in his seat.

"Not long." Jada twists in her seat. "Were you dreamin'? You were mutterin' to yourself." Her voice is low, because Ashara, next to her, is asleep.

"Yeah." Luke stares out of the window: they're turning off a dual carriageway, into an industrial estate. The sun is still high, the clouds sparse. They pass a factory, the gates of which are half open. A single lorry sits in the forecourt, its tailgate open, with three dead bodies on the ground close by. *When did seein' shit like that become normal?* The flutter of a company flag on the roof catches his eye; he notices smoke on the wind. "Where are we?"

"Not far from the camp."

"Is this the estate off the ring road?"

"Yeah. Near the prison. Not long now, an' we can have a rest."

"We've earned it."

"Yep. We won't stay too long. Just need to get Lena well. Then we can go to your dad's. If that's okay with you?"

"Sure. 'Ow's she doin', Lena?"

"She's alright, I think. The first dose wouldn't be enough on its own, but the IV drip should do the trick."

"We're actually gonna make it, aren't we? All still alive, goin' somewhere safe, 'n' you get to tell yer story."

She reaches over the seat and takes his hand. "We are. It's like a film, or somethin'. Horrible, terrifyin' events, but the bad guys get what's comin' to 'em, 'n' the good guys walk away."

"Hand in hand, into the sunset." He squeezes her fingers.

"Into the sunset. Maybe, when everything's settled down, we can, ya know, go for a drink, or somethin'?"

"That'd be awesome. Somewhere other than Manchester, though, obviously. If the outbreak's not spread. Whole country could be fucked."

"Could be. But I reckon they'll get a handle on the situation, at some point. Get more troops in, maybe foreign intervention. They've gotta do *somethin'*. Can't just let millions die."

"No. They can't." Luke looks at his son, who's now talking to Evie. The two children laugh at something. They've been excited about going to the refuge since the choice was made, as is Theo, but not Gabriela. She's like Floyd, vigilant, her gaze flitting from one side window to the other. *No, they can't let millions die. So many kids like Connor 'n' 'is new friend, left without one or both parents. Or dead themselves. Or undead, turned into animals, wonderin' the streets, lookin' fer other humans to kill, 'n' eat, then be killed themselves.* He shudders. "It's all just so… fucked up." Watching the pavement as they drive, slowly due to the volume of abandoned vehicles on the road, he sees a bloody-faced dead man gorging itself on something out of view. The bus's passage gains the monster's attention for a moment, but it soon loses interest and returns to its feast. Luke's disquiet is fleeting; he's becoming inured to such things. "Will there ever be a 'normal' again, d'ya think?"

"Yeah. It won't be the same 'normal' we used to have, but it'll be better than this."

The bus is decelerating. It turns left at a hastily-erected sign promising that Manchester Refugee Camp is two hundred and fifty yards away.

"I told you!" exclaims Gabriela.

What now? Groaning at the creak of his knees, Luke stands and shuffles down the aisle towards Gould. The smoke he saw earlier is thicker up ahead. Emanating from the fenced compound at the end of the street, the fumes are dark, those of a petroleum or diesel fire.

Gould wears a pained expression. "Not a good sign, is it?"

Now everyone's standing, gathering at the front of the bus, pointing.

"Told him what?" asks Luke, facing Gabriela and Theo.

The latter looks sheepish. "She was talkin' 'bout the smoke. But she couldn't have known it was comin' from the camp, could she?"

"I *knew*." The teenaged girl isn't triumphant, though. "I told you that, an' I was right. This is a bad idea."

She elected to go to Luke's father's house, and the closer they get to the perimeter fence, the more judicious her vote appears.

On the other side of the gates, two lorries have crashed into one another. The yard in front of the distribution warehouse is littered with bodies. Two plumes of smoke, one dark, the other grey, stream from the wide, low building. Tongues of flame caress the wall to the far right, where a dumpster is on fire. Glass from breeched windows glitters in the westering sun. Scraps of clothing strewn across the tarmac shift in the breeze.

But nothing is *moving*. Whatever has occurred is already finished; they're seeing a ghost of events.

Perhaps this is just a minor outbreak. This could still be a temporary sanctuary fer us, till we move on t' m' dad's. If we shoot the corpses t' make sure they don't get up. There might still be food 'ere, beds, doors we can lock. Maybe even a few survivors, 'idden away. 'N' the gates are shut. So the attackers came from within. If there are zombies still 'ere, inside, we can kill 'em. Make the place safe. All's not lost.

The gunshots shatter his illusions.

"This is a bad idea," Gabriela repeats.

Printed in Great Britain
by Amazon